As she walked out ahead of him, he noticed a sparkling diamanté clip holding her hair up at the back.

A light but evocative scent of roses and something a little spicier caught his nostrils. It hinted at the sensuality she was hiding under her *Who, me?* surface.

It wasn't usual for Zach to be taken by surprise by anyone or anything. It had happened once and never again. Even though it had been only a couple of minutes in time, four years ago, he'd never forgotten her—not her face or how she'd felt pressed against him. Her soft mouth on his jaw... Her scent, clean and fresh...

So different from the women he'd found himself surrounded by as his success had grown. As he'd become a man who was desired and sought after. As he'd become a target.

Ashling Doyle had reminded him that night that he was always going to be a target. She clearly had no idea of the damage her actions had done.

But she would.

Abby Green

THE FLAW IN HIS
RED-HOT REVENGE

HARLEQUIN
PRESENTS

ISBN-13: 978-1-335-56792-5

The Flaw in His Red-Hot Revenge

Copyright © 2021 by Abby Green

This edition published by arrangement with Harlequin Books S.A.

For questions and comments about the quality of this book,
please contact us at CustomerService@Harlequin.com.

Harlequin Enterprises ULC
22 Adelaide St. West, 40th Floor
Toronto, Ontario M5H 4E3, Canada
www.Harlequin.com

Printed in U.S.A.

Irish author **Abby Green** ended a very glamorous career in film and TV—which really consisted of a lot of standing in the rain outside actors' trailers—to pursue her love of romance. After she'd bombarded Harlequin with manuscripts, they kindly accepted one, and an author was born. She lives in Dublin, Ireland, and loves any excuse for distraction. Visit abby-green.com or email abbygreenauthor@gmail.com.

Books by Abby Green

Harlequin Presents

Awakened by the Scarred Italian
The Greek's Unknown Bride

One Night With Consequences

An Innocent, A Seduction, A Secret

The Marchetti Dynasty

The Maid's Best Kept Secret
The Innocent Behind the Scandal
Bride Behind the Desert Veil

Rival Spanish Brothers

Confessions of a Pregnant Cinderella
Redeemed by His Stolen Bride

Visit the Author Profile page
at Harlequin.com for more titles.

This is especially for Anne McAllister—I told you
I'd get "Eamon" into a book one of these days.
Now all you have to do is find him! xx

PROLOGUE

ASHLING DOYLE WAS so nervous that she was taking short panting breaths and it was making her light-headed. She had to force herself to take deeper breaths. She just hadn't expected this place to be so…intimidating.

She was tucked behind a large plant, hidden from view, in one of London's most iconic and historic hotels, which was hosting one of the city's most exclusive events in its annual social calendar.

Even the air smelled expensive. She'd only realised a short while before that it was scented, which added to the very rarefied atmosphere and the gobsmacking luxury of the place.

She touched her hair again nervously, even though the wig felt secure. She wasn't used to long hair tumbling over her shoulders in sleek waves. Or the vibrant red colour that gave her a jolt of shock whenever she caught a glimpse of her reflection.

She shivered slightly when someone opened a door nearby and the frigid winter air touched her exposed skin. Of which there was a lot. She looked down at the tight black strapless dress and tried to tug it ineffectually higher over her breasts. It sat an uncomfortable few inches above her knees and it sparkled when she moved, from the crystal embellishment in the material. Discreet, it was not.

She spoke to the man in the suit beside her, Carter. She'd only met him this evening and he had given the spec for the job. He would supervise her. 'Every other woman is wearing a long evening dress…won't I stick out?'

Carter flicked her a glance. 'It's perfect. Remember you're playing a part. You're not a guest here.'

As if she needed reminding that she didn't belong in a place like this, and would never, in normal circumstances, be mixing with this rarefied crowd. But then, this was not a normal circumstance. She was only here as a massive favour for a friend from her amateur dramatics group, who couldn't make it.

She looked back out to the crowd through a gap in the foliage. 'That's him? The man in the middle? With the dark brown hair?'

In a classic black tuxedo, he shouldn't be standing out from hundreds of other men similarly dressed but he did. And not just because he was taller and broader than everyone else. It was something the eye couldn't see, but which Ashling could sense even from this distance. Power. Charisma. Sexual magnetism.

'Yes, that's him. He's talking to a blonde woman.'

A prickle of foreboding went up Ashling's spine. There had been no mention of a woman.

Carter took her arm and thrust her out from behind the plant and towards the crowd. 'This is the moment. Do it now.'

Ashling hesitated.

He spoke from behind her. 'If you don't go now the moment will be gone and you won't get paid.'

Ashling's belly lurched. She needed the money to finish her yoga teacher training course or she'd never establish herself. She took a deep breath to quell her nerves and threaded her way through the crowd until she was right behind the man.

He seemed even taller up close, almost a foot over her very average five foot five. And she was wearing heels. His back looked impossibly broad and imposing. His suit was lovingly moulded to his powerful body as only a bespoke suit could be.

Ashling had no idea who this man was—only that he was the one she had to target with the script she'd been given. An elaborate practical joke, she'd been told. She'd put it down to the crazy whims of rich people, who did strange things because they could...because they were bored.

She wasn't going to get anywhere looking at his back, so she stepped around him and stood right in front of him.

And promptly lost the ability to breathe and form a coherent thought.

He was...breathtakingly gorgeous. Short dark hair, dark eyes, and an unashamedly masculine bone structure. Hard jaw and high cheekbones softened only by a surprisingly sensual mouth, a lush lower lip.

He'd been smiling at the tall blonde woman by his side, but now the smile faded as he looked at Ashling. His eyes dropped, taking in the dress which Ashling realised had been picked for exactly *this* effect.

Even though it had a designer label, she stuck out like a tacky bauble amongst clear bright gems. The woman beside him was wearing a white dress, cut with the kind of elegance that could only be manufactured by hand in an atelier in Paris. Ashling registered all this without even looking at the woman.

'Just stick to the script and then leave.'

The words of instruction came back to her. She came out of her trance and nerves started to bubble upwards.

Emptying her mind of everything but the role she was playing, Ashling launched herself at the man, wrapping her arms around his neck. *'There* you are, darling, I've been looking everywhere for you.'

She pressed a kiss to his jaw—the only part of his face she could reach. Her lips came into contact with granite-hard bone and stubble. Her body was pressed against a wall of steel and flesh. His scent filled her nostrils—deep and woodsy, with a hint of something more exotic, causing a quiver of sensation in her belly. More than a quiver. A wave. It was such a shock to find herself reacting with this much intensity that she froze.

The man put his hands on her arms and pulled them down, unpeeling her from his body, pushing her back but not letting her go. His face was thunderous. 'Who the hell are you? I've never seen you before in my life.'

Ashling didn't have to call on any acting skills to portray her dismay. His touch wasn't harsh, but his expression and tone were horrified. She'd known to expect exactly this reaction—after all she *was* a complete stranger to him—but she hadn't counted on his response affecting her so viscerally. It made no sense.

She blinked and felt moisture gather under her lashes. His gaze narrowed. She said, in a tremulous voice that she didn't really have to manufacture, 'But, darling, last night was the most amazing night of my life. You told me I was special. How can you say you don't know me?'

For a split second Ashling wondered what it would be like to have a man like this tell her that she was special. Then she lambasted herself, disgusted at getting caught up in dangerous fantasy even for a moment. This kind of man, this kind of place, was not her world and she never wanted it to be. It had rejected her a long time ago.

Out of the corner of her eye Ashling could see the woman in white go rigid. Dimly she wondered about their relationship, but she'd gone too far now.

'What the hell...?' he said now, sounding genuinely mystified. 'You are a complete stranger to me.' He looked her up and down again, cold disdain etched all over his face. 'I would never touch a woman like you.'

Ashling went cold all over. Suddenly she forgot why she was there. All she knew was that she was standing in front of a man who fascinated her and who had a powerful effect on her. And who was rejecting her.

Echoes of another, too similar situation came back to haunt her... Approaching a man in the crowd. Tapping him on the shoulder. Him turning around. Him not recognising her. She'd had to tell her own father that it was *her*—his firstborn daughter. His illegitimate daughter.

At first there had been no recognition and then, slowly, comprehension had dawned. And with it not surprised delight, as Ashling had hoped, but horror. He'd grabbed her arm, pulling her away. Aside. Out of sight...

Ashling pushed the memory down where it belonged, hating it that this situation was precipitating its resurgence. But the tendrils lingered, and irrational hurt at this stranger's response made her pull free of his hold. She could never have suspected that this incident would be a trigger for her. But she was triggered. And caught between two worlds.

She tried desperately to focus on the job at hand, but the recent past and present were meshing painfully as she said, 'So now, here with your friends, I'm not worthy of you?'

His lip curled. 'You're talking nonsense—you don't belong here.'

The inexplicable hurt inside Ashling solidified, making her want to protect herself. Words that she wasn't even aware of formulating fell from her mouth. 'From what I recall, there wasn't much talking last night. How many times did we *not talk*? Two? Three? You told me I was the best you'd ever had.'

There was an audible intake of breath from someone. The blonde woman? Ashling couldn't break free of that dark gaze. A breeze skated over her exposed skin, making her shiver. Sanity trickled back slowly.

She realised that she'd gone way beyond the original spec and that she had about a second before the man reacted and her very flimsy disguise was exposed for the sham it was.

She lifted her chin. 'I know when I'm not welcome. I'm good enough to take to bed, but not to stand by your side in your world.' Tears gathered, because she felt that sentiment down to her very bones. She wasn't acting any more. Her vision turned blurry. 'You just used me because you were bored, or jaded, or…something. Well, I'm worth more than that.'

She turned and pushed her way through the silent crowd, trembling with the overload of adrenalin and emotion. Emotion that had no place here.

She went straight up to the suite where she'd changed beforehand. Carter was waiting. She ripped the small microphone from under the bodice of the dress and handed it back to him. She felt nauseous as the full impact of what she'd just done sank in.

Carter was grinning. 'You did a great job—the ad-libbing was a brilliant touch. We have a Murder Mystery Weekend coming up in a castle in Scotland…you'd be perfect for it.'

Ashling recoiled at the thought. 'I only did this because Sarah wasn't feeling well. It's not really my scene.' In fact, she wasn't sure she'd want to keep up the amateur dramatics after this.

The man looked her up and down, and Ashling didn't like the assessing gleam in his gaze.

'Shame, you're a natural.'

He handed her an envelope full of cash. 'This might help change your mind.'

Ashling looked at the envelope, suddenly reluctant to take it. It felt tainted. Dirty. She said, 'This was meant to be a practical joke…it didn't feel like a joke.'

Carter's eyes narrowed. 'You're the one who turned it into something else. You only had two lines to deliver and then you were meant to get out of there.'

Shame rose up. He was right. She'd overreacted and over-acted because she hadn't expected the man to affect her like that. She hadn't expected his rejection to feel so personal.

She asked, 'Who is he anyway?'

Carter shrugged, bored. 'Just some billionaire. Believe me, he'll have already forgotten about you.'

That stung more than she liked to admit. 'Then why hire someone like me in the first place?'

Carter's expression hardened. 'I don't ask questions when someone wants to hire one of my actors for a private event, once I know there's no funny stuff involved. This was one of the easiest jobs. Who knows why people do the things they do?' He thrust the envelope at her again. 'It's money for old rope—now, take it and go. If you want more gigs like this, you know where I am.'

Ashling took the envelope, but when she was walking away from the hotel a short while later, minus the wig and dress, back in her own clothes again, she felt sick. She was passing a homeless shelter, and on an impulse she couldn't ignore she went in and handed the money over to the manager.

He looked at it and her with shock. 'Thank you, miss, are you sure?'

She nodded and fled, putting the whole evening down to an unsavoury experience not to be repeated. She thanked her lucky stars that she would never meet that man again.

CHAPTER ONE

Four years later...

IT WAS A warm late summer's evening and Ashling Doyle was half walking, half running down a Mayfair street, white stucco houses towering over her on each side. She imagined all the windows were like eyes, judging her for sullying this exclusive part of London with her bedraggled, sweaty self.

She felt a bubble of hysteria rise up from her chest, but she pushed it back down. It was only masking the severe anxiety that had been gnawing at her insides since her best friend Cassie had asked her to do her a favour. A very doable, innocuous favour.

All she had to do was pick up and deliver a tuxedo to Cassie's boss for a function that evening. She couldn't have refused. Not when she knew her friend's PA was out sick and Cassie was under pressure—she'd left London earlier that day to go to the United States for a two-week work trip.

Ashling also couldn't have refused because Cassie would have wondered why on earth she couldn't do this really minor little thing.

But Cassie had no idea why this was not a minor

little thing. It was huge. And it was the reason why, ever since Cassie had started working for her boss, and had then worked her way up the ranks to become an executive assistant, Ashling had always found an excuse not to come to Cassie's workplace or attend any social work events.

Cassie had put it down to Ashling's distaste for all things corporate and regimented.

But that wasn't the reason why Ashling had to avoid Cassie's boss. Zachary Temple. A man who had single-handedly become one of the most powerful financiers in the City of London. Temple Corp dwarfed every other financial institution with its innovative ways and ruthless ambition.

Zachary Temple was the man the government called on for help. He was the man who, with a click of his fingers, could make economies falter. And what he could do for the companies he invested in didn't bear thinking about unless he thought they were worth it.

He was also, far more importantly, the man who Ashling had hoped never, ever to meet again. The man she had confronted at an event four years ago, when she'd been just twenty years old and dabbling in amateur dramatics.

She'd only realised who he was when Cassie had pointed out a picture of him in a newspaper, saying, 'That's him! That's my new boss.'

Ashling had told her friend about that night after it had happened, but of course she hadn't had a name for the man then. Now she did. A feeling of sick dread had sunk into her belly. Guilt. She hadn't had the guts or the heart to tell Cassie that *he* was the man she'd publicly shamed for no good reason.

Her guilt and shame had only grown over the years, as Cassie had spoken of Temple in hushed, reverential tones. She'd never been able to understand Ashling's antipathy or studied lack of interest in the man. 'Wow, he really gets up your nose, doesn't he, Ash?' her friend would say. 'You've never even met the man!'

But it didn't stop Cassie blithely tell Ashling about his legendary attention to detail, which extended beyond the office to his personal life, and to the women he carefully chose to take as his lovers—none of whom seemed to last long.

Ashling could recall only too well the woman at his side that evening, and she'd barely glanced at her. Tall, Hitchcockian blonde. Refined. Sophisticated. Everything Ashling hadn't been that night. And still wasn't.

She slowed to a walk. Temple's house was in front of her now. It stood on its own among other houses. A detached townhouse in the middle of London would be worth more money than she could earn in about ten lifetimes. Not to mention, according to Cassie, Temple's palatial country home outside London, his penthouse apartment in Manhattan and his pied-à-terre in Paris.

Ashling doubted she'd amass enough money in this lifetime even to buy a modest studio flat. Oh, she earned enough money to support herself, and she was proud of her independence. But her payment came in in fits and starts, due to the nature of her myriad revenue streams.

Trepidation pooled in her belly at the thought of seeing the man face to face again. At the thought that he might somehow recognise her, even though she looked nothing like she had that night four years ago.

She had blonde bobbed hair, currently pulled back into a messy ponytail. No make-up. Athleisure wear instead of a black minidress. She still cringed when she thought of all the other women that night, in their long evening gowns.

She forced herself to walk up the steps. As it was, she was late with the tuxedo, and she did not need to add fuel to her reputation for scattiness, which Ashling always thought it was a bit unfair—until Cassie invariably pointed out the numerous occasions when Ashling's attention to detail had been somewhat lacking. Like the time she'd left Cassie sitting in a restaurant for an hour because she'd been so engrossed in a book at the library. Or when she'd forgotten to stock up on milk. Or missed her bus stop because she'd been too busy daydreaming.

She shoved aside the reminder that she was behaving true to form and regarded the massive matt black front door in front of her. It was flanked on either side by small potted trees. She instinctively reached out and touched a leaf, to see if they were real, and at the same moment the door opened—which was just as well, because Ashling hadn't seen any sign of a bell or knocker.

She blinked at the uniformed butler. He looked exactly the way she would have imagined a stern, silver-haired butler to look.

'Good afternoon—' She winced inwardly. 'I mean, *evening*. I'm Ashling Doyle—Cassie…er… Cassandra James's friend—Mr Temple's executive assistant? She asked me to bring a suit for him, for an event.'

Ashling lifted her arm to indicate the suit draped over it in its protective black zip-up bag.

She could have sworn she saw the butler wince as

he reached for it, saying, 'Mr Temple is most anxious for this as he's already late—'

'Peters, was that the door? Is that the damn girl with my tuxedo?'

Ashling's insides dropped at the censorious tone. She'd hoped that she would be able to get away without seeing him.

At that moment Zachary Temple appeared behind the butler, towering over the older man, who was saying, 'Yes, sir, it's your suit. I'll deliver it to your suite right away. The car will be in front in fifteen minutes.'

Ashling was left standing in the doorway, looking up into the forbidding features of Zachary Temple, who was as darkly gorgeous as she remembered. She felt as if she was trapped in the blinding beam of powerful headlights. Unable to move. His dark eyes were totally unreadable, just as they'd been that night four years ago.

She didn't see a spark of recognition, and wasn't sure if she was relieved or disappointed—ridiculously. *Not disappointed*, she assured herself. She definitely did not want this man to recognise her.

He seemed taller than she remembered. Broader. The muscles of his biceps bulged from beneath his black polo shirt sleeves and the open buttons drew her eye to the bronzed column of his throat. His chest was wide, and the shirt did little to disguise taut musculature underneath.

The thick dark hair was still kept almost militarily short but even with that she could see that it had a tendency to curl. And for some reason that detail made her pulse trip even faster. His jaw was as hard as granite, and at that moment she recalled how his stubble had felt against her lips when she'd pressed her mouth there.

But then he spoke. 'You'd better come in—you look hot.'

Ashling blinked, as if coming out of a trance, and became all too conscious of her 'hot' state. She'd all but run here from the local tube station. She must be a sight in her three-quarter-length joggers, sneakers, and a bra top under a loose singlet. It was, after all, still close to thirty degrees on a hot London summer evening.

No wonder he didn't recognise her...

But she couldn't risk it by hanging around. She backed away. 'It's fine. Cassie just wanted me to deliver the suit and I have—'

'About an hour late.' Zachary Temple looked pointedly at the watch on his wrist.

A shiver skated over her skin as she recalled how he'd looked at her before and said, *I would never touch a woman like you.*

Ashling stopped in her tracks. She bit her lip. A nervous habit. 'I'm sorry... I was on my way to the dry cleaners straight after my class, but one of my students—'

Temple frowned. 'Students?'

'I teach yoga.'

He said nothing to that, so Ashling did what she did best whenever an awkward silence grew. She filled it.

'Like I said, I was leaving to go straight to the cleaners, but one of my students started having a panic attack, and I had to wait with her and help her breathe through it, and then I stayed with her until her boyfriend came to collect her… I couldn't leave her on her own in that state.'

Temple arched an unamused brow. 'Isn't yoga meant to have the opposite effect on people?'

'Actually, a practice or class can bring up a lot of emotions for people.'

He looked at her as if she'd just spoken in an incomprehensible dialect. But then he stood back from the door. 'You should have some water—you look like you need it.'

Contrary to what her head was telling her to do— which was politely decline and leave, and hopefully not lay eyes on this man again for at least a decade— Ashling found her feet moving forward and into the hushed and blessedly cool entrance hall of Zachary Temple's home.

It was a huge space, with a black and white chequered marble floor leading up to a central staircase. The sunlight caught the crystals of a massive chandelier overhead and sent out shafts of iridescent light just before Temple shut the door behind him, effectively muting the sounds of the city.

He must have telepathically communicated to a member of staff, because at that moment a maid in a black short-sleeved shirt and trousers appeared and handed Ashling a glass of water with ice and lemon.

'Thank you…' She took it from the young woman, who then vanished back down a corridor—presumably to wherever the kitchen was. She took a gulp to try and cool down.

Ashling wasn't used to being around someone as coolly impassive as Temple. She was an animated person and generally used to putting others at ease—

the benefits of a peripatetic upbringing with a single mother who'd had a tendency to befriend total strangers.

She risked a look at him, to find him staring at her as if she was some kind of alien object. No wonder… He was used to mingling among people who looked a lot more put-together. She couldn't imagine Cassie, for instance, appearing before Temple in anything less than her sleek, elegant, business-suited perfection.

'You live with Cassie…you're her childhood friend.'

He stated this and Ashling nodded, mentally cursing her friend for asking her to do this favour. 'Yes, we've been friends since we were eight. My mother worked for her father as his housekeeper for about five years, so we lived together.'

Ashling blushed when she thought of how that sounded. 'Well, obviously not "together" like equals, because Mum and I lived in a flat in the basement beside the kitchen, but Cassie never made me feel *less than*—even though she went to the fancy day school and I went to a different one…' She trailed off. She was gabbling again.

'I really should let you get on with your evening, Mr Temple. I've delayed you enough. Sorry about that again.'

Ashling drained the icy glass of water in one go, which gave her brain-freeze for a few seconds. As she looked around helplessly for somewhere to deposit the glass Temple said, 'Here, I'll take it.'

She handed it to him and their fingers brushed against each other. The fleeting physical contact made Ashling jerk her hand back so fast that the glass almost slipped between their hands to the marble floor, but Temple caught it.

Before she could react to that, he said, 'The delayed tuxedo isn't my only problem.'

Ashling looked at him. 'What do you mean?'

He looked even more unamused now. 'Cassie's PA—Gwen—was meant to come with me to the function this evening, to take notes. Obviously she can't as she's unwell.'

'Oh, of course…' That was why Ashling had been drafted in to pick up the tuxedo at short notice.

Abruptly Temple asked, 'Can *you* take notes?'

Ashling had not been not expecting that. Almost automatically she responded, 'I've worked as a temp and a secretarial assistant—of course I can take notes.'

'Then you'll come with me this evening.'

It took a few seconds for what Temple had just said—announced, actually—to sink in.

'You want me to come with you?' Ashling's voice was a squeak. She balked at the thought of such a preposterous suggestion. At the thought of going anywhere with this man who she should be avoiding at all costs. Any more time spent in his company risked him recognising her.

'You did Cassie a favour by bringing the tuxedo… late, I might add…but without Cassie or her PA I'm still down a member of staff for the evening.'

At that succinct summary, Ashling couldn't think of anything to say. She had no plans for the evening other than to sip a cold glass of rosé while reading a good book on the terrace of the flat she shared with Cassie, but that looked elusive now, when she thought of Cassie, blissfully unaware of the fact that her boss was not happy.

Also, Ashling didn't really relish the prospect of Cassie getting to say *I told you so* when she found out about the delayed tuxedo. If she did this then surely the delayed tuxedo would be forgotten and all would be well again?

'I… Okay, I guess… If you really need someone.' She couldn't have sounded more reluctant.

Temple's dark, unreadable gaze looked her up and down. 'Do you have anything to wear? It's black-tie.'

Ashling went cold all over as she was reminded of that sparkly black dress. Too short and too tight. But, as it happened, she did have some clothes with her.

Cassie was due to attend a fancy wedding in San Francisco on her arrival in the States, and as her self-appointed stylist—because she knew more about fashion—Ashling had found her some options of outfits to choose from. She still had the rejected dresses in her bag as she'd been planning on returning them to the vintage shop, and luckily they had the same size feet.

And, as much as Ashling was tempted right now to say, *no*, she didn't have anything to wear, in a bid to get out of accompanying Temple, her innate honesty, coupled with her desire to prove—even just to herself—that she could be counted on, made her say, 'I do, actually. But it's a cocktail dress. Would that be suitable?'

'That'll be fine.' Temple headed towards the marble staircase. 'Follow me. I'll show you to a guest suite where you can get ready.'

She followed him up the stairs, her eyes on the broad back narrowing down to slim hips. The material of his black trousers hugged his buttocks as if tailored just to fit his muscular contours.

She almost ran into those muscular contours when he stopped suddenly at a door. She hadn't even realised they were in a long corridor, plushly carpeted in slate-grey, with doors leading off either side.

He opened the door and stood back. 'You can use this suite.'

She walked in, taking in the opulent luxury of the room.

He said from behind her, 'Have we met before? Perhaps with Cassie?'

Ashling was glad she was facing away from him, so she could school her features before she turned around. 'No,' she said, while mentally crossing her fingers, 'I've never met you with Cassie.' Which, technically, was not a lie. She *hadn't* met him with her friend.

He looked at her for a long moment, as if not entirely convinced. Then he glanced at his watch again. 'You have fifteen minutes. Come down when you're ready.'

The door closed and Ashling sagged. He hadn't recognised her. Now all she had to do was get through this evening and hope that nothing sparked his memory.

He'd recognised her as soon as he'd laid eyes on her.

Zachary Temple paced back and forth in the reception hall a short time later. Anger bubbled in his blood. Anger and something a lot more disconcerting.

Awareness.

The moment he'd seen her standing in the doorway, in spite of the fact that her hair patently *wasn't* long and flowing and red, the sense of déjà-vu had almost knocked him over.

He'd sworn he'd never forget that oh-so-innocent face and those huge blue eyes…that lush mouth that had stayed emblazoned in his mind for days afterwards.

And he hadn't.

He wasn't sure how he'd managed to contain his rage just now, but it had taken levels of control he hadn't had to call on since he was a teenager, being goaded by the school bullies because he'd been an outlier in their midst.

Ashling Doyle was *her*. The mystery woman who had appeared and disappeared like a faery sprite four years ago, teaching him an important lesson in never being complacent and always watching his back.

That night four years ago Zach had been publicly humiliated. Exposed. His years of working so hard to prove himself had almost come to nothing. His success had still been a fragile thing, easy to dismantle. He'd had to work twice as hard to build his reputation back up again. Restore people's confidence in him.

He never would have known that the friend Cassie spoke of so fondly as she described her various scatty escapades was the same woman who had left such a trail of destruction in her wake.

The two women had known each other since they were children. What did that say about Cassie? He trusted her implicitly, but if this woman was her friend… He went cold inside at the thought that she might know.

He suddenly regretted his impetuous decision to take Ashling Doyle with him. To toy with her. He didn't have time for this. He should have confronted her straight—

But then he heard a sound from behind him. He

turned around slowly, the back of his neck prickling with some kind of strange foreboding.

There was a woman standing at the top of the stairs in a black silk dress, and for a second Zachary wondered who the hell this stranger in his house was—before he realised it was her.

She was coming down the stairs slowly, because of her vertiginous black heels. His eyes travelled up from her feet, taking in slim calves and a toned thigh, peeking out from the slit in the dress. Gone were the hot pink Lycra leggings and the yellow singlet worn over an even more lurid purple sports bra.

She was transformed.

Cinched in at her waist, black silk clung to her breasts and then went over one shoulder, leaving the other bare. A vivid pink flower was pinned to the dress at the waist on one side. Her skin was lightly golden. Her hair was pulled back into a rough chignon, showing off the delicate bone structure of her jaw and face. Subtle make-up made her eyes huge, her lashes long and dramatic.

But it was her mouth that Zach couldn't take his eyes off. The mouth that he remembered so well.

It took a second before he realised the sound of roaring in his head was his blood.

He told himself it was anger. Not desire.

But he shouldn't be surprised. After all, he'd seen her transformed before.

He looked at the flower. It should look gaudy, but somehow…it worked.

She looked nervous—which was patently an act.

She gestured towards the flower. 'The dress just felt a bit…too black. I can take it off.'

That caused a vivid image of this woman stepping out of the dress, standing there naked, to enter Zach's mind. He cursed it and said frigidly, 'It's fine.'

She said, 'I've left my things upstairs... I'm not sure what to do with them.'

Suspicion coursed through Zach's veins. She was already sizing up the opportunity this turn of events had afforded her. He was doing the right thing. He wanted to see just how long she would keep up this charade.

'Leave them there. You can pick them up later or we can arrange to have them delivered back to you.'

'I don't want to cause more hassle...'

He curbed an urge to laugh at her theatrics. She really was very plausible. But then she'd had four years to hone her skills.

Zach put out a hand to indicate that they should leave. 'My driver is waiting.'

As she walked out ahead of him he noticed a sparkling diamanté clip holding her hair up at the back. A light but evocative scent of roses and something a little spicier caught his nostrils. It hinted at the sensuality she was hiding under her *Who me?* surface.

It wasn't usual for Zach to be taken by surprise by anyone or anything. It had happened once and never again. Even though it had only been a couple of minutes in time, four years ago, he'd never forgotten her—not her face, or how she'd felt pressed against him. Her soft mouth on his jaw... Her scent clean and fresh...

So different from the women he'd found himself surrounded by as his success had grown. As he'd become a man who was desired and sought after. As he'd become a target.

Ashling Doyle had reminded him that night that

he was always going to be a target. She clearly had no idea of the damage her actions had done.

But she would.

CHAPTER TWO

ASHLING'S HEART WAS still pounding after the effort it had taken not to tumble down those marble stairs in the high heels and land in a heap at Zachary Temple's feet, and more so from the dark, brooding appraisal he'd subjected her to.

At every step down the stairs she'd imagined that he would be remembering who she was, and her skin had prickled all over with little needles of heat that she'd put down to self-consciousness, not awareness.

But he hadn't said anything. And, actually, when she thought about it now she realised it was really delusional of her to fear that he would remember her. Why would he, when it had been so long ago and he was habitually surrounded by the most beautiful women in the world?

How on earth would Ashling have made any kind of impression, except perhaps as an annoying fly that had had to be swatted aside?

Ashling was not his type. He'd looked at the flower she'd pinned to the dress as if it was a live thing. She'd seen his type. Tall, sleek, soignée... Cold. Oozing class and sophistication. They wouldn't be pinning flowers to their dresses to liven them up a bit.

The women a man like Temple pursued would have the right breeding and the intellect to match. Like him, they would have been born into this world—a world that didn't accept people from the margins. She should know.

His type of woman would have had a privileged and conventional path to success. Her CV wouldn't have an education littered with gaps and holes. Not to mention a list of myriad jobs such as Ashling had had over the years, none of which could be considered conventional.

But then, Ashling had never been destined to be conventional. Her single mother had loved Ashling fiercely and had taught her how to be independent and believe in herself. She'd believed in the school of life ethos—and Ashling had certainly seen a lot of life, going from living in a palatial house in Belgravia to living on a commune in the west of Ireland.

But convention and things like a solid base had not been her mother's priorities. Angela Doyle was a dreamy romantic who had taken a long time to get over the hurt and pain of rejection by Ashling's father.

But right now, sitting in a car next to one of London's giants of industry, was not the time for Ashling to be dwelling on her lack of credentials or thinking of painful memories. She just had to get through this evening and not cause a national incident. Or make him remember her and that night.

She sneaked a look at Temple, sitting on the other side of the car. She'd seen him in a tuxedo before, but the impact this time was not diminished. If anything, four years seemed to have enhanced his physicality. Her gut tightened at the sheer raw masculinity of the man. There was nothing soft about him. Not his expression, his bone structure, or his body. Just that intriguing tendency of his hair to curl.

No wonder she'd had to cling to the banister the whole way down those stairs. The man needed to come with a health warning. *Proceed with caution. May cause severe dizziness!*

He looked at her then, as if aware of her regard, and Ashling could feel the heat climb up her chest. In a bid to try and deflect his attention from her helpless reaction, she asked, 'What is the event this evening?'

'It's an awards ceremony for young entrepreneurs.'

'Oh, cool.'

He arched a brow. *'Cool?'*

As if Ashling needed reminding that she was so not his type. And glad of it.

Liar.

'I mean,' she said, aiming to sound knowledgeable, 'that should be interesting…seeing the next generation of talent…or competition?'

A ghost of a smile flickered at Temple's mouth so briefly that Ashling knew she must have imagined it.

He said, 'Competition for me? I don't think so.'

She might have thought he was joking if he hadn't sounded so utterly matter-of-fact. It went beyond arrogance to total certainty. And she knew he didn't joke. He didn't have time. Cassie had told her about his work ethic. This was a man who had his whole life mapped out.

Normally that kind of rigidity would disgust her, but she found she was more intrigued than anything.

'What exactly do you want me to do?' she asked.

He glanced at her. 'Listen…observe. Take notes.' Then he asked, 'You said you're a yoga instructor?'

She nodded.

'*Just* a yoga instructor?' he commented idly, quali-fying it with, 'I can't imagine teaching yoga alone is enough to keep the wolf from the door.'

Ashling shivered slightly, but put it down to the air-conditioning in the car and not the sudden image she had of a slightly more wolfish Zachary Temple ap-pearing at her door. Her imagination was far too vivid for its own good.

Conscious of her colourful CV, Ashling felt slightly defensive as she answered. 'No, it's not my only job, although I do consider it my main one. But, I also wait-ress in a local café. And I do some styling work for dif-ferent clients.' They were friends, but Cassie had told her that referring to them as clients made it sound more important. She went on, 'I also care for an old lady who lives in our building for a few hours a week—do her shopping…things like that.'

'Anything else?'

Ashling looked at Temple. She sensed she was amusing him. It made her prickly. 'Yes, as it happens. I did a course in cordon bleu cookery along the way, but I'm sure the minutiae of my CV really isn't that interesting.'

Something stretched between them—a tension that made Ashling nervous, because it felt charged with something she couldn't understand. And then it was broken when Temple looked over her shoulder.

'We're here.'

Ashling turned her head to see that the car was pull-ing up outside one of London's most iconic museums. Paparazzi lined a red carpet and A-list stars mingled with politicians and household names from the business world. One she recognised was from a well-known TV show, in which budding entrepreneurs were pitted against each other.

Well, this was one experience she'd never had…

She tried to quell her nerves as the driver came around to open her door. Temple was already waiting for her. He put out a hand to help her and she looked up at him for a moment. She was suddenly very reluctant to touch him, afraid of her reaction, but she couldn't ignore him.

She was right to be afraid. As soon as her hand touched his, electricity scorched up her arm. The palm of his hand was rough, not smooth. Not the soft hand of a man who sat at a desk all day. But then, she already knew there was nothing soft about him.

For a moment he just looked at her, almost as if he hadn't seen her before, but then he let her hand drop. He said, 'Stay close to me.'

Ashling had no intention of letting him out of her sight. As the reality of the situation sank in, she grew more terrified. The paparazzi were screaming out for people to turn and smile for them. She heard Temple's name being called but he ignored them, cutting a swathe through the crowd of preening people as if they were minions and not some of the biggest names in the country.

They had almost run the gauntlet of the red carpet when someone jostled Ashling from behind and she pitched forward. Even though Temple was ahead of her, he turned at that second and caught her as she collided with his body.

It was like running into a steel wall. The shock of contact drove the breath from her lungs.

He held her arms, looking down at her. 'Okay?'

She managed to nod, even as a wave of unbridled heat coursed up from her core and out to every erogenous zone. Exactly the way it had felt four years ago. An immediate rush of sensation, hot and overwhelming. No man had ever had the same effect on her—not before or since. In fact, she'd believed in the intervening years that she'd imagined it.

But it hadn't been imagination.

It had been very real. Powerful.

Her hands were splayed across Temple's chest, under his jacket. She wanted to press herself closer, but she exerted enough pressure to straighten herself, feeling hot and flustered. She felt a tugging neediness between her legs…an ache. Her breasts were bare under the silk of the dress because she hadn't had a suitable bra, and they felt tight, her nipples pricking into hard points against the sensuous material.

She took her hands down, avoided his eyes. 'Sorry about that. I… I lost my balance.'

For a moment Temple didn't move, and the air hung suspended between them as people passed by. She felt an icy finger touch her back. *Did he recognise her?*

But then he moved, manoeuvring her so she was in front of him.

Ashling told herself she was being ridiculous.

He put a hand lightly to her back, propelling her forward and into the lavishly decorated venue, where hundreds of people were already chatting, networking and sipping sparkling vintage champagne.

Ashling sucked in a shaky breath.

* * *

She was playing with him.

Zach felt a mixture of anger, consternation and very unwelcome arousal as he kept a hand lightly on Ashling's back as they walked into the function room.

That little stunt just now had been designed to let him know how her lithe curves felt pressed against him. Exactly the way she'd momentarily robbed him of his logical faculties for a dangerous moment four years ago. Giving her the chance to do her damage and get away.

The fact that she still had an effect on him was galling in the extreme. So was the fact that he could be caught by someone so full of guile.

As for the myriad occupations that she'd listed earlier... No doubt they'd been plucked out of thin air to disguise the fact that she only really had one job: con woman.

But he knew who she was now, and he wasn't going to be caught again. She wouldn't slip through his fingers this time.

Ashling sat down with a sigh of relief after what had felt like hours of trailing in the wake of Temple and his Midas Touch. He'd met with hundreds of sycophants, all vying for his attention.

The novelty of being on the other side of the red rope, so to speak, had worn off fast. The man's energy levels were indefatigable, and it had taken all her wits just to keep up and try to take notes on her phone.

There'd also been a steady stream of stunning women. All tall, statuesque, and exuding a sexual confidence that Ashling found both intimidating and fascinating. None of them had even spared her a glance. That was how little of a threat she was.

Ashling slid off her shoes under the table now and stretched her feet out. She stifled a yawn. Her busy day was catching up with her. She'd been up since five that morning and had packed in more than was usual, even for her. And that had been before the trauma of seeing Temple again and worrying that he'd recognise her...

'Are we boring you?'

Ashling looked to her right, where Temple was taking up far too much space. She smiled sheepishly. 'Sorry, it's been a long day.'

His dark gaze moved to her mouth and for a moment she couldn't breathe, remembering pressing her mouth to that hard jaw. The scent of him. Earthy and spicy all at once.

She blinked and Temple looked away, his jaw clenching. Ashling cursed herself again for being so weak. *Ugh.* What was wrong with her? She was disgusted with herself for finding him so mesmerisingly attractive when he inhabited a world she had no desire to explore.

Her father had been a successful financier—albeit nowhere near the league of someone like Temple. He had rejected Ashling and her mother because they hadn't fitted into his corporate world. They'd cluttered it up. Made it untidy. And so he'd jettisoned them in favour of a far more acceptable wife and family.

What Ashling had learned about Temple from Cassie had only reinforced the impression she'd got of him that night four years ago. That he had nothing but disdain for anything or anyone who put a wrinkle in the perfect surface of his life. The way he'd looked at her that night—with such horror. She'd never forget it.

It still hurt.

She shoved that memory down, rejecting the fact that it still had the power to affect her.

'Mr Temple? We need you backstage now, on stand-by to present the first award.'

A woman in a suit had appeared, breaking Ashling's circling thoughts.

Temple got up, buttoning up his jacket. He slanted a look to Ashling. 'Don't go anywhere now, will you?'

There was a distinct edge to his tone that made her nervous, but when she looked at him his expression was bland. She was imagining things. She shook her head and watched as he walked away with such innately athletic grace that every head and set of eyes was pulled in his direction.

Temple was up on the dais now, and people were clapping. At that moment Ashling had the fleeting thought of doing exactly what he'd just asked her not to. Get up and leave. Escape. Consign him to history, where he'd safely been until this evening.

But at that moment, as if hearing her thoughts, Temple's gaze stopped on Ashling. His focus was so intense that she saw people turning to look at her, wondering who he was staring at.

The whole way through his speech Temple barely took his eyes off her. There was absolutely no chance of her going anywhere. He'd as good as branded her.

'Really, you can just drop me at a tube station. I can come by tomorrow to pick up my things.' Ashling was still jittery after Temple's intense focus during his speech. She wanted to get out of his disturbing orbit.

'It's after midnight. You're not taking the tube alone at this hour.'

Ashling refrained from telling Temple that she'd been taking late-night tubes on her own for some time now. She was street-smart. His tone brooked no argument and they were already back in the leafy exclusive streets of Mayfair.

He'd undone his bow-tie and the top button of his shirt and it was hard for Ashling not to look at him and notice how the stubble along his jaw and the loose bow-tie gave him a decadently sexy air. It added to the brooding energy that was almost palpable.

The car pulled to a smooth stop outside the house, and before Ashling could step out Temple was at her door, opening it and holding out his hand. She steeled herself, but it was no good. As soon as they touched, skin on skin, electricity pulsed up her arm and into her blood. She took her hand away as soon as she was standing.

He led her into the house, where all was dimly lit and hushed. Ashling suddenly felt self-conscious. Very aware of how he made her feel and the fact that he must be dying for her to go. As much as she was dying to leave! she assured herself.

'I'll just run up and change and get my things.'

Temple was pulling off his tie completely now, and undoing another button with long fingers. 'Take your time. The car will be waiting to take you home when you're ready.'

Ashling slipped off her shoes and hurried up the stairs, the marble cool under her bare feet. When she got to the luxurious suite she looked in dismay at the minor explosion she'd created when getting ready earlier.

She wasn't the tidiest person on the planet. And she wasn't used to wearing much make-up. So she gave in to an impulse to clean her face in the sumptuous bathroom. And then she saw the massive shower…and remembered that the shower in the flat she shared with Cassie was currently on the blink. A plumber was due to come tomorrow.

The lure of this massive state-of-the-art shower and the chance to wash off the grime and humidity of the day was too tempting. Assuring herself it would only take five minutes, Ashling stripped off and groaned softly as she stepped under a gloriously hot, powerful cascade of water.

Where the hell was she?

Zach put down his empty tumbler and looked at his watch. She'd been upstairs for thirty minutes now. It hadn't taken her that long to get changed earlier.

Frustration rising at himself for playing this game, letting her feign innocence and a lack of recognition, rose like fire inside him. She was probably upstairs laughing at him.

The thought of that propelled him out of the room, up the stairs and to the door of the guest suite to seek her out and—

Zach stopped on the threshold of the room.

Ashling was emerging from the en suite bathroom in a wave of steam. She wore nothing but a short towelling robe. The hem rested high on her thighs, showing off more of her slim shapely legs than he'd seen earlier. It was belted around her slim waist and the front gaped open slightly, giving a glimpse of the curve of a breast. Pale and plump.

Immediately Zach had an image in his head of her naked body in the shower, water sluicing over slender limbs, curves and pert breasts. Firm buttocks.

Desire was swift and hot, eclipsing the anger that had propelled him up here. He was rendered momentarily insensible. He couldn't remember the last time a woman had precipitated such intense need.

She hadn't seen him yet. She was rubbing at her damp hair with a smaller towel.

In that moment Zach clawed back control with an effort and fresh anger rose as he interpreted the scene.

Ashling only sensed she wasn't alone after she'd stepped into the bedroom and a crackling tension in the air skated over her skin. Her hands went still and she looked up to see Temple standing in the doorway, without his jacket, waistcoat and tie, the top buttons of his shirt open. But even the shock of seeing him standing there couldn't diminish her first helpless reaction—pulsing awareness and a flash of fire in her belly.

'I was wondering what was taking you so long,' he said, with no discernible tone to his voice.

Except Ashling fancied she could hear a steel undertone.

The full impact of having been found like this hit her, and an awfully familiar wave of guilt and shame overwhelmed her. She was trespassing. She didn't belong here. She saw the chaotic detritus from her bag strewn all over the pristine suite. Shoes on the floor near Temple's feet.

She took down the towel from her head and said, 'I'm so sorry. I saw the shower and I couldn't help myself. The shower in our flat is broken and it's been a long day and—'

'You don't need to explain. After all you did me a favour this evening, joining me at short notice.'

Ashling's mouth shut. Temple had stepped into the room. The door was still open behind him. Her skin prickled with heat as his dark gaze rested on her. The air suddenly felt thick with a kind of tension Ashling had never experienced before. It coiled tight in her gut. Down low.

She was very aware of her naked body under the robe.

She opened her mouth again, tried to form something that sounded coherent. 'I… It was the least I could do…for Cassie. I'm sorry I was late.'

Temple took another step into the room. He shrugged. 'We got there in time. It was really no big deal.'

Gone was the stern Zachary Temple, and in his place right now was someone Ashling found far more disturbing. His gaze dropped momentarily. Ashling realised the robe was gaping open.

Embarrassment warmed her face as she pulled it together. 'I should really get going. I've imposed enough.'

'There's no rush…is there?'

Ashling looked at Temple, wondering if she'd misheard him. Why did she feel as if every limb was weighted down and she couldn't move? Didn't want to…

All she could see was him. Those impossibly broad shoulders. His hard jaw, dark with stubble, like it had

been four years ago. The sensation of how it had felt
under her lips was still vivid.

Oh, God. Now was not the time for memories. Not
when past and present were colliding in a way that was
seriously disorientating.

Then he said, 'You felt it between us, didn't you?
From the moment we met?'

Ashling's mouth went dry. She'd been that obvious?
'I...um...what do you mean?' But her heart betrayed
her, beating fast.

Temple's mouth quirked into a little smile. 'Do you
really want me to spell it out?'

When had he moved so close that she could almost
touch him? So close that she could smell his scent?
Deep, and dark, and musky. Infinitely masculine.

And then mortification coursed through her when
she realised that he hadn't moved another inch towards
her. She'd moved towards him without even realising.
As if pulled by some invisible force.

Temple's gaze dropped to her mouth and then down,
before coming back up. 'You're a beautiful woman.'

Her eyes widened. She struggled to find her voice.
'I'm nothing special.'

'I disagree.'

This from the man who had once looked at her and
said, *'I would never touch a woman like you.'* That
memory still scored away at her insides, even though
she'd told herself that she was over it.

Temple repeated his words. 'You feel it too, don't
you? This heat between us.'

Ashling was fast losing any sense of reality or desire to think coherently. Was Temple really saying he

fancied her? Asking her to admit she fancied him too when it had to be laughably obvious?

Before she could articulate a word, he reached out and touched his fingers to her jaw. A touch so light she could barely feel it, and yet it burned like a brand. He traced the line of her jaw, his fingers under her chin, his thumb exploring her lower lip.

Ashling's breath was coming fast. She was drowning in a sea of melting sensations, desperate for Temple to bring her closer. Her eyes were fixated on his mouth, wondering what it would feel like on hers... She didn't recognise herself right now. She'd believed that she didn't have much of a sex-drive.

But at that moment Temple took his hand away and stepped back, his face shuttering. A small sound of pleading came out of Ashling's mouth. She barely noticed.

He said, 'I'm sorry. I misread the signals. I thought you were attracted to me too.'

It was such a reversal to hear this man say he found her attractive that it took her a second to realise that he thought she didn't fancy him. Ashling blurted out, 'No—*wait*. I mean... I am attracted to you too...'

Temple stopped. 'Are you sure?'

Ashling nodded and took a step closer, a boldness she'd never felt before giving her confidence. Confidence born out of this man admitting he wanted her.

She said, 'Please... I don't know...'

I don't know what to do.

She couldn't admit that she didn't know what to do. How did one behave with a man like Temple? He was so tall. Broad. Intimidating. He must be used to worldly lovers, taking the lead, showing him exactly what they wanted.

'Do you want me to kiss you?'

Relief mixed with excitement flooded Ashling's body, making her tremble. She nodded. Temple stepped closer. He lifted a hand and cupped Ashling's jaw again, his fingers caressing the back of her neck under her damp hair.

Gently, he tugged her closer, until their bodies were almost touching. He looked down at her. Tipped her chin up. Lowered his head. Ashling's eyes fluttered closed as Temple's mouth hovered for an infinitesimal moment before closing over hers.

Nothing she'd imagined or held in her memory since that night four years ago could have prepared her for this…this immediate rush of sensations. Melting heat at her core, blood rushing to her head, and an urgency to get even closer, have him kiss her harder.

She didn't even realise her hands had tangled in his shirt, pulling him even closer. Her mouth moved under his, restless, seeking a deeper intimacy. And he obliged, coaxing her lips apart so that he could explore and deepen the kiss until Ashling was no longer conscious of anything but this exquisite moment in time.

With one hand at the back of her head, holding her so he could plunder her mouth, Temple drifted his other hand down along the front of the robe Ashling wore, his fingers teasing along the edge, close to her bare skin. Ashling's breath quickened under his mouth, where he held her captive to his masterful onslaught.

He pushed the robe aside. Ashling could feel cool air skate over the bare skin of her breast. She pulled back from the kiss reluctantly, opening her eyes. Temple was out of focus. She was breathing heavily. He was cupping her breast now, his eyes on her there. A thumb stroked her nipple. She could feel it tighten into a hard bud of need. She almost whimpered.

He looked at her as he teased her flesh. 'What is it? What do you want?'

Ashling bit her lip. Then she blurted out, 'I want you to touch me...'

Put your mouth on me.

She didn't have the nerve to say that. She was reeling from the fact that apparently she *did* like being made love to. That her previous experiences hadn't defined her.

Temple's fingers trapped her nipple. 'Here? This is where you want me to touch you?'

She nodded.

He smiled and it was wicked. 'You really want this?'

Ashling nodded. Almost feverish with lust. Begging silently.

Then he said lazily, 'I wondered how far you'd go...'

He was bending his head, his breath feathering close to her exposed skin, his mouth coming ever closer to her straining nipple... But something cut through the heat haze in Ashling's brain. Words that she hadn't really understood. A tone that made her uneasy.

She tensed. Pulled back.

Temple straightened up, his hands dislodged.

Instinctively she pulled the robe over her exposed breast. 'What do you mean by that?'

CHAPTER THREE

TEMPLE FOLDED HIS arms across his chest. She noticed then that he barely had a hair out of place, when she felt hot and dishevelled.

He said, 'You really don't have to put on this act, Ashling. The game is up. I know exactly who you are. I recognised you as soon as I saw you—and for what it's worth, the red wig was not a good look.'

Ice landed in Ashling's gut, dousing the feverish lust. *He'd known all evening.* She'd suspected, but she'd convinced herself that he couldn't possibly…

As if she had to hear him confirm it, she said faintly, 'You knew?'

He nodded, grim. 'Your face was etched into my memory after that night. I swore if I ever saw you again you'd pay for what you did.'

Ashling felt sick as the full magnitude of what had just happened sank in. He hadn't been making love to her because he fancied her. He'd been toying with her, giving her enough rope to hang herself. And she'd been well on her way to doing just that.

Temple started to walk around her. 'Based on previous experience, I might have expected you to be waiting in my bed, naked.'

The thought of being naked in his bed made a million conflicting things rise up inside her, chief of which was a betraying surge of excitement.

He was in front of her again. She said, 'Of course I wouldn't do something like that.'

Temple arched a brow. 'Why not? When you're halfway there with this little stunt?'

'It wasn't a stunt. I really did just want to have a shower. There wasn't anything else going on.'

Until he walked into the room and told you he fancied you and you were all over him in seconds.

Ashling wanted the ground to open up beneath her feet and swallow her whole.

Temple made a dismissive sound. 'Somehow, when you've already pretended to be my jilted lover, it's not such a stretch to suspect you'd be willing to go even further,' he said. 'You cost me a lover that night, and a lucrative deal. Tell me…how much did it earn you?'

You cost me a lover. Ashling didn't like how that impacted on her, deep inside. That woman had meant something to him…

She shook her head. 'You don't know how sorry I am about what I did. I was just following instructions. I didn't even know your name. I was filling in for a friend. I never did anything like that again.'

Ashling's conscience pricked. She could remember how his rejection of her had made her go off-script, because it had impacted her on a personal level, reminding her of her father's rejection.

All she'd had to do was pretend to be his lover and then flounce out when he issued the expected denial. But she'd been caught—trapped by those dark eyes, his words of denial and rejection cutting far deeper than she'd expected.

She forced herself to ask, 'Did your lover really leave you?'

Temple's mouth was a hard line. 'What did you expect? You put on a very convincing act of knowing me intimately. Not many women would put up with public humiliation. Do you know who put you up to it?' he asked abruptly.

Ashling shook her head. 'It was a casting agency—I knew the girl who was meant to do the job because we were in an amateur dramatics group together. She was sick that evening and asked me to do it in her place at the last minute. I don't know who hired the agency.'

'I do,' Temple said tersely. 'It was someone looking to undermine my reputation and derail a deal. But until now I thought you were a call girl.'

Ashling gasped in shock. 'I am not a call girl.'

He was grim. 'Could have fooled me.'

For the first time in her life Ashling felt a surge of anger so hot it almost blinded her for a moment.

'Don't even think about it...' Temple warned.

Ashling realised her hands were clenched into fists at her sides. Shock at the very notion that she might commit violence made it drain away as quickly as it had surged.

No one had ever had this effect on her.

She felt acutely vulnerable as the memory of how he'd looked at her four years ago meshed painfully with the last few minutes. It had been a cruel lesson, designed to humiliate and punish her.

She pulled the edges of the robe together over her chest. 'Look, I'm sorry about that night. It was irresponsible of me to step into a situation that I didn't know much about. If it's any consolation I felt terrible afterwards, and I gave the money they paid me to a homeless shelter.'

Temple wasn't impressed. Or most likely didn't believe her. 'I couldn't care less what you did with the money. I want to know what you thought you were going to get out of *this* situation.'

Ashling gasped as his very clear implication sank in. '*You* came in here. *You* kissed me.'

'After making sure it was what you wanted. I wanted to see how far you would go.'

She would have gone all the way. That realisation scraped painfully along her still sensitised nerve-endings.

She said, 'I did not come here this evening for any other reason than to do a favour for my friend.'

Temple looked stern. 'How involved is Cassie in this?'

Dread gripped Ashling at the thought that her actions might have consequences for her friend. '*She's not.* She knows nothing about what happened.' She clarified. 'I mean, I told her about that night at the time, because I felt so bad about it, and I knew it wasn't right, but she never knew that you were the man involved. *I* didn't even know until she showed me your picture in the paper.'

Zach looked at the woman in front of him. Cassie was one of his most trusted employees. Right now she was in the United States, scoping out a potential investment prospect for him. The thought that he'd entrusted her with so much information and the possibility existed that she was in league with this woman would be a betrayal of the worst kind.

As if reading his mind, Ashling Doyle said, 'Please, Cassie doesn't have any idea that we've met before. She knows nothing at all.'

She looked genuinely tortured. Face pale. It was conceivable that Cassie know the extent of her friend's machinations. She was loyal. Or at least he'd always believed so. Maybe that loyalty had blinded her to her friend's true nature.

Cassie would be back from the United States in two weeks. He would have to give her the benefit of the doubt for now, but he resolved to discuss it with her on her return. First he had to deal with *this*.

Much to his intense irritation, his blood was still running too hot for him to think clearly. He'd only intended to kiss Ashling Doyle, to see how she'd react, but as soon as he'd touched his mouth to hers he'd started to lose control of the situation.

The memory of the feel of her breast in his palm, firm and plump, was still vivid enough to entice him over the edge again. As was the memory of that kiss. Her soft mouth under his had been tremulous at first, and then growing bolder.

She said she wasn't a call girl. Her faux naive ways told a different story. Gallingly, his attempt to prove how far she was willing to go had only proved to him that she still had a very unwelcome effect on him. *That he wanted her.*

Disgust at his own weakness made him feel exposed and angry. Too many revelations for one evening.

He moved back and said curtly, 'Get dressed and get out of my house, Miss Doyle.'

* * *

Ashling looked at the empty space left behind Zachary Temple for a long moment, unable to move. She had a moment of hoping that maybe she'd just experienced a very vivid hallucination. But, no, her mouth was still tingling and she could still feel his hand on her breast.

It was shocking how quickly he'd made her forget everything. Who she was. Where she was. He'd barely touched her and she'd gone up in flames.

She'd believed it was a myth that desire could consume one so utterly. She'd had two short-lived relationships and they'd only confirmed her belief that that kind of desire didn't really exist. Or didn't exist for her.

But Temple had blown that assumption out of the water.

She just hadn't met *him*.

His curt dismissal hung in the air, and Ashling had a vision of him returning to find her still standing there like someone transfixed. She moved quickly, changing into the first things she could find, not caring if they matched, stuffing the rest of her clothes into her bag.

As she went downstairs she held her breath, dreading the thought of seeing Temple again. But there was no sign of him. The butler materialised, looking seriously disapproving. What was his name again? Peters? He couldn't possibly know what had happened, but she felt as if he did.

He opened the front door, saying coolly, 'Mr Temple's driver is waiting to take you home.'

Ashling's insides curdled at the thought of being any more beholden to him than she already was. 'Thank you, but I don't need a lift—'

'Mr Temple insists.' The butler's tone brooked no argument. Not unlike his boss.

Feeling shame and guilt and mortification all at once, Ashling exited the house and went down the steps. The driver was waiting by the open back door of the car. She heard the front door of the house close behind her with a distinct *click*. Another feeling joined the cauldron swirling in her gut: the all too familiar one of having trespassed where she didn't belong.

She was tempted to plead again that she didn't need a lift, but the driver looked nice and she didn't want to get him into trouble.

She thanked him as she got in, and within seconds he was executing a neat U-turn in the street and driving her away from the man she knew she'd never forget. Not now. Not now she knew how he tasted. How he felt up close. Holding her. Touching her. And it had all been a cruel act to humiliate her. To prove that she was something she wasn't.

If she'd been able to think clearly she would have pretended that she was equally unmoved. But it was too late for that now.

To try and distract herself she took out her phone and saw a message from Cassie, who must have arrived in the United States by now.

You were right about the dress, Ash. I'm not even the most naked woman here... But what happened with the tux? You had one job, Ash!!

Ashling quickly typed a perky reply.

It was a little late, sorry! Everything okay in the end.
Don't worry and enjoy the wedding! Xx

She groaned and let her head fall back. She was so
busted.

The following day Ashling was gritty-eyed, after a
night of broken sleep dominated by scary dreams in
which she'd been in a room full of people looking for
someone…looking for *him*. When she'd finally found
him the relief had been intense. She'd put a hand on
his arm but he'd turned around and looked down at
her, saying coldly, 'Take your hand off me. I would
never touch a woman like you. You don't belong here.'

Now, Ashling switched the heavier shopping bag to
her other hand. She didn't need to be a genius to know
that meeting Temple again, and the fact that he'd recognised her, was bringing up all her insecurities and
deeply buried fears. Stuff she didn't even talk to Cassie
about as it felt too pathetic.

Like the fact that she'd never really felt she belonged…anywhere. Hence her very haphazard life,
working at about a million different jobs to see if
anything fitted. *Or felt like home.* And the fact that
she wore bright, eclectic clothes as a sort of rebellion
against her instinctive need to fade into the background
in a bid to please her father so he might accept her.
Even after all these years.

She scowled. She hated Temple even more now. For
what he was. For what he'd done to her last night.

You were with him all the way…begging, reminded
a little inner voice.

She scowled harder in rejection of that, even though

it was true. Mostly she hated Temple for making her feel vulnerable. Exposed. For reminding her of the guilt she'd always carried since that night. Except she had no one to blame for that but herself.

She was so busy thinking about Zachary Temple that when he got out of the back of the same sleek car that had driven her home last night all she could do was blink at him. He looked completely out of place in the quiet, leafy residential street, in a steel-grey three-piece suit. No less impressive than he'd been in a tuxedo.

Ashling blinked again, sure that her too-vivid imagination was playing tricks on her. Especially after that dream. But he didn't disappear.

All she could think of to say was, 'Are you really here?'

His grim expression told her that he most likely was real. She became very aware of her pulled back hair, make-up-free face, three-quarter-length bright blue joggers, flip-flops and pink tank top. She'd been planning a yoga practice after returning from the shop.

He held something out. She looked at it. It was a shoe. One of the shoes she'd been wearing last night. She must have left it behind in her rush to change and get out of Temple's house.

Ashling cringed. She was no Cinderella, and he probably thought she'd left it behind on purpose.

She couldn't take it as her hands were full of bags of shopping. She put one down, feeling flustered. He'd hardly come just to give her a shoe. She reached out and took it, pushing it into one of the bags, uncaring if it cracked an egg.

She stood up again. 'You didn't have to come all the way here. If you'd let me know I would have picked it up.' She could imagine Peters, the butler, handing it over, pinched between his fingers, as if it smelled bad.

'It was on my way.'

Ashling looked at him, still too stunned to move, even though they were right outside the house where she shared the ground-floor apartment with Cassie.

Temple said, 'We need to talk. We can do it here, or…?'

Ashling's pulse tripled at the thought of him in her apartment, but they couldn't stay standing in the street. She could already see curtains twitching.

She moved past him, saying reluctantly, 'Please, come in.'

She thought she heard a dry, *I thought you'd never ask…'* from behind her, but she couldn't be sure.

She opened the front door and immediately a thin voice floated down from the floor above. 'Is that you, Ashling dear? With my shopping?'

Ashling called up, 'Yes, Mrs Whyte. I'll bring it up now.'

She looked at Temple, who had a bemused expression on his face at this little domestic exchange. Did the man ever smile? she wondered snarkily. And then she remembered him smiling seductively before he'd kissed her. Maybe it was better that he didn't smile.

She put down the bags and opened the door into her and Cassie's flat, saying, 'I need to take Mrs Whyte her shopping first. It'll just take me a few minutes, if you don't mind. She gets anxious.'

Temple pushed open the door with a finger and stepped over the threshold. 'Please, don't keep Mrs Whyte waiting.'

Ashling took the stairs two at a time with the shopping for her neighbour. She took as long as she imagined would be tolerable to keep a man like Zachary Temple waiting, her insides churning as she tried to figure out why he was here.

When she returned to the apartment Temple had his back to her. He was looking at a framed photo collage that hung on the wall near the fireplace.

He pointed to a photo without turning around. 'This is you and Cassie?'

Ashling knew without checking which photo he was looking at. A picture of her and Cassie, arms wrapped tight around each other, pulling faces.

'Yes, we were about ten.'

It was her favourite photo of them. There were also pictures of her and her mother, with her bright red dyed hair piled high on her head and heavily lashed blue eyes, wearing a kaftan and ornate earrings. Her mother's typically understated attire. *Not*. It had embarrassed Ashling as a child who had just wanted to fit in, but now she was proud of her unorthodox mother. She'd come through so much on her own.

She became very conscious of the apartment as Temple would see it. The crystals in the windows, sending out little rainbows of light across the walls and ceiling. Plants populated almost every corner. Her yoga mat was on the floor. There was a large Buddha statue in the corner, where the stick of incense that Ashling had lit earlier was almost burned through, leaving the scent of sage in the air.

Feeling panicky, Ashling said to Temple's broad back, 'What can I do for you, Mr Temple?'

He turned around, looked at her, and said, 'I want you to come to Paris with me.'

* * *

Ashling was looking at him as if he'd grown two heads. Zach kept his gaze *up*, even though he wanted to let it rove over her lithe body, where nothing much was left to the imagination, with Lycra clinging to slim curves.

The lurid clashing colours of her clothes did little to detract from her appeal. Even though her hair was pulled back and she wore no make-up, she really was extraordinarily pretty.

Last night she'd been beautiful.

And sexy.

Sexy enough to make him lose his mind for a moment.

Sexy enough to make him almost forget who she was, what she'd done, and what she owed him.

A debt.

A debt he had every intention of calling in.

He knew it wasn't entirely rational to take her to Paris with him, but his every instinct was screaming at him to keep her close. Where he could keep an eye on her. In case she ran before he felt she'd paid her due.

Not because he wanted her. He had more control than that.

That ill-judged attempt to see how far she would go if he were to push her, hadn't been enough in terms of satisfying his thirst for revenge over what she'd done.

She'd wittingly—or unwittingly, according to her— exploded a bomb in his life at a time when he'd been most vulnerable. In many respects he'd had to start over again. Prove that he was reliable. Not out of his depth, or a dilettante. Since then his liaisons with women had been carefully judged and discreet. And his work ethic left no room for error.

Eventually she said, 'Of all the things you could have said to me, that is literally the last thing I would have expected. Why on earth would you ask me to come to Paris with you?'

Yes, why would you? asked a voice that he ignored. He knew what he was doing.

'Because you owe me a debt and this is how you'll pay it off.'

Ashling went very still, and then her eyes widened and her cheeks flushed with colour. 'I told you I'm not a call girl.'

Her outrage was authentic. Zach could see that. He said coolly, 'I'm not suggesting you pay off your debt in my bed. I have an important meeting in Paris and I need someone to come with me as an assistant. As I'm without Gwen and Cassie, you can save me the trouble of going through HR to find someone else at short notice on the weekend.'

The colour had receded a little from her cheeks now. 'You want me to act as your assistant?'

'It's the least you can do.'

She started to get agitated, moving around. It only drew Zach's eye to her slim form.

'Look,' she said, 'I've said I'm sorry. That night I was doing someone a favour... I knew it was unorthodox, but I had no idea of the repercussions. I was young and naive. I should have known better. I'm sorry.' She stopped moving and looked at him, beseeching. 'But I can't just drop everything and go to another country with you because you demand it.'

Zach looked around, taking in the surprisingly homely apartment. The scene didn't entirely fit with his image of her as a con woman—or a call girl, for that matter. But then, perhaps Cassie's influence was the dominant one here.

There was a comfortable couch. A massive TV. Books on shelves. He could imagine Ashling curled up on the couch, engrossed in something. There was a yoga mat on the floor, the lingering smell of fresh coffee in the air, and something he couldn't identify. Something New Agey.

To his surprise, it caused a pang in his chest. Brought back a memory of his mother standing behind him, her hands on his shoulders as she'd said, 'Look around you, Zach. *This* is not where you belong. You belong far from here. You belong in a place that the people here will never see in their lifetimes. But you will, because it's your due.'

Zach clamped down on the memory, irritated by its resurgence. He glanced at his watch and looked at Ashling. 'You have fifteen minutes. I'll be waiting in the car. We'll return this evening.'

He was almost at the door when she said, 'Now, wait just a minute—'

He turned around. '*No*. You owe me, Miss Doyle, and I'm collecting. If what you say is true, that Cassie knows nothing of this, and you want to keep it that way, then you'll do as I say.'

She went pale. 'That's blackmail.'

'Fifteen minutes or I'll come and get you. Dress smartly.'

Ashling spent five minutes after Temple had left the apartment pacing up and down and vacillating between anger at his arrogance and fear that he would tell Cassie what she'd done.

Ashling could imagine the look of disappointment on her friend's face. Cassie had never hidden the fact that she thought Ashling had gone over a line that night, and it had only compounded Ashling's own feelings of guilt and remorse. Cassie had worked so hard to get to where she was. She had a great relationship with Temple, and Ashling would hate to damage that.

So, if anything, the fact that Temple was offering her a chance to prove that Cassie wasn't involved and redeem herself...was a good thing. They would be quits.

She cringed, though, when she thought of the first place her mind had gone when he'd mentioned Paris. *Bed. Sex.* And the rush of very conflicting reactions in her body. Shock. Relief because he did fancy her. Excitement. And only then disgust at what he was insinuating. That she could pay him back *on* her back.

But he hadn't meant that at all. Because he didn't fancy her. As if she needed reminding.

She stopped pacing. She could see the sleek car outside the window. Imagined Temple sitting in the back, growing impatient. She really didn't have a choice. She couldn't bear to see the disappointment on Cassie's face. Or, worse, get her into trouble. He was right. She did owe him. This much at least. After a day in her company no doubt he'd be only too happy to see the back of her.

When Ashling got into the back of the car approximately ten minutes later. Temple gave her a once-over and as the car pulled away from the kerb. 'What are you wearing?'

Ashling felt defensive. 'You said to dress smartly.

This is smart.' *For her*. She'd even borrowed one of Cassie's cream silk shirts with a pussycat bow.

Temple was looking at her lap. 'Is that a leather mini-skirt?'

'It's fake leather,' Ashling replied, indignant that he would assume it was real.

She'd paired the skirt with black sheer tights with black dots and flat leather brogues. For her, this was positively conservative.

Temple's gaze went to her head. He said dryly, 'I'm sure my French counterparts will appreciate the authentic touch.'

Ashling resisted the urge to take off her jaunty beret. 'I'm sure they will.'

She put the briefcase she'd also borrowed out of Cassie's wardrobe on her lap. She'd stuffed in notebooks and pens, not sure what would be required of her.

In a bid to try and distract herself from the enormity of the fact that she was going to Paris for a day with Zachary Temple, Ashling asked, 'So what exactly is the meeting about?'

'You don't need to worry about the details. You'll be making sure everyone has water…that kind of thing.'

Ashling smarted at his dismissive tone—but then this was payback.

She said, 'I have the notes from last night on my phone. If you need them I can transcribe them.'

He frowned. 'Notes?'

'That's why you asked me to accompany you yesterday evening…' But then something occurred to her and she cursed her naivety. 'You didn't need notes taken at all, did you? You just wanted to watch me squirm because you knew who I was.'

Temple didn't even look remotely sorry.

At that moment his phone rang and he took it out of his inside pocket, answering and proceeding to conduct a conversation in fluent French, which made him sound even sexier than he usually did. Even when he was being hateful.

Ashling scowled and looked out of her window, willing the day to be over already.

Ashling had never been on a private jet before. She'd naively assumed they would be taking the train to Paris. But, no, they'd driven to a private airfield beside one of London's biggest airports, where a gleaming silver Learjet had been waiting.

It was seriously plush inside. Cream leather seats. Luxurious carpets. Temple settled in without a second glance, opening up his laptop. Ashling hovered, unsure what to do…totally intimidated.

Temple looked at her. 'What's wrong?'

'Nothing.' She chose a seat on its own by a window. Her phone buzzed from her—from *Cassie's*—briefcase, and Ashling took it out, relieved to have something to do with her hands. It was another text from Cassie, and Ashling's eyes widened as she read it. Cassie had apparently slept with the man she'd gone to the States to spy on.

Ashling sneaked a glance at Temple, in case he could somehow magically read the text from a few feet away—she wouldn't put it past him—but he was engrossed in his laptop. She fired back an incredulous response, telling herself that Cassie obviously had enough on her plate to be dealing with, without hearing about Ashling's temporary new job as Temple's assistant.

She put the phone away. One of the stewards came over when they were in the air. 'Would you like some champagne, Miss Doyle?'

Ashling blanched. Maybe that was what was offered to Temple's usual companions. Women he brought with him for far more recreational reasons. Not for punishment. 'Er...no, thanks. Water would be fine. Or, coffee, if you have it.'

She would need all the help she could get to stay alert around the most disturbing man she'd ever met.

CHAPTER FOUR

'HAVE YOU BEEN to Paris before, Miss Doyle?'

Ashling tensed and turned away from the car window, where she'd been sighing at the sight of the Eiffel Tower in the distance. 'You can call me Ashling. "Miss Doyle" makes me sound like a schoolteacher.'

'Very well. Ashling.'

She immediately regretted saying that. He hadn't even called her Ashling last night, when he'd been making love to her. *Humiliating her.*

But then he said, 'You can call me Zach. I don't usually stand on ceremony with employees.'

A neat reminder—as if she needed it—that her initial assumption that he meant to bring her to Paris to sleep with her was about as likely as her becoming CEO of a company some day.

'So, Ashling, have you been here before?'

She swallowed, not liking how hearing him say her name made her feel. 'Just once before, with my mother. For my eighteenth birthday.'

Her romantic mother had told her that she should see the city with someone who loved her, even if it was her mother, so that her first impression of the most beautiful city in the world would always be remembered with love.

She could be grateful of that experience now, considering she was here with someone who didn't feel remotely romantic about her.

'You've obviously been here a lot. You speak fluent French,' Ashling said.

'I have an apartment here,' he responded.

Of course, Cassie had told her. Yet he wasn't staying the night. She wondered if he had a lover at the moment.

The car pulled to a stop outside one of the world's most iconic hotels. Ashling saw glamorous women in designer dresses with sleek hair and discreet jewellery walking in. One woman led a tiny beautifully groomed poodle on a jewelled lead.

She suddenly felt self-conscious in her attempt at a 'smart' office outfit. No wonder he had looked at her the way he had. She took off the beret and stuffed it into the briefcase. She'd thought it was cute and quirky. Now she realised she looked ridiculous. All she needed was a string of onions around her neck and a stripy top.

The driver was at her door and she stepped out with as much grace as she could muster. Zach was waiting, and moved forward when she joined him. She had to almost trot to keep up with him.

A man who looked as if he must be the manager hurried over as they walked into the lobby. Zach exchanged a few words with him and then the man said to Ashling, 'Anything you need, Miss Doyle, call my personal number.'

He handed her a card and she took it. Zach was

already at the lift and she ran to join him just as he stepped inside.

When the lift stopped another suited man was waiting for them as the doors opened directly into what Ashling assumed was the penthouse suite. The views were astronomical. The Eiffel Tower was so close she felt she might be able to touch it. A large boardroom table had been set up in the main living area. A group of men and women, all suited and looking very serious, were waiting for Zach.

Ashling could see that bottles of water were on another table, with glasses stacked up, so she started busying herself by putting them out. One thing she'd learnt in her years of multi-jobbing: *use your initiative and keep busy.*

Zach cast an eye around. He seemed to note what Ashling was doing and said grudgingly, 'Good. We're just waiting for a couple more people—can you make sure they know where we are?'

'Of course.' She was more than happy to escape.

She went out into the lobby area just as a man and woman were arriving. They barely glanced at her as she told them where to go. Then there was no one for a few minutes. Starting to feel bored, Ashling did a little rearranging of the fresh flowers in a massive vase on a round table, humming to herself.

She heard a noise behind her and turned around to see an older gentleman getting out of the lift. He'd dropped his briefcase and papers were all over the floor. With a little exclamation Ashling rushed forward and bent down, helping him to gather them up.

She could see that he was slightly out of breath and,

worried that he might be unwell, led him over to a chair to sit down. He had a kind face and he smiled at her. She tried to communicate in broken schoolgirl French but he put up a hand.

'I speak English.'

He had an accent she couldn't quite place. European, but with a slight American twang.

Ashling smiled. 'Are you okay? Would you like some water?'

'That would be lovely. Thank you, my dear.'

When she came back he was looking much better. She handed him the water. 'Is there anything else I can get you? I presume you're here to meet Zachary Temple?'

He nodded and handed her back the empty glass. 'That's all I need.'

He looked at her and she could see the shrewd twinkle in his eye.

'Who are you? We haven't met before.'

'Oh, I'm no one—just someone filling in for Mr Temple's assistants. Please, let me show you to the meeting room.' The man got up, and as Ashling led him into the penthouse she said with a little wink, 'I have the personal number of the manager, so let me know if you need anything else.'

The man grinned. 'I will do, my dear.'

Zach appeared at the door leading into the living area. He greeted the man with enough deference to make Ashling wonder who he was. But then they disappeared, and Zach closed the door behind him, leaving Ashling firmly on the other side and in no doubt as to what her position here was.

Firmly on the outside. Not that she cared.

* * *

Hours later, after the last guest had left the suite, dusk was colouring the sky outside a bruised lavender. As much as Ashling wanted to go and sigh over the view, she knew she wasn't there for that. She busied herself clearing up discarded papers and cups of coffee and plates from the snacks and food that had been delivered all day.

'You don't have to do that.'

Ashling turned around to see Zach in the doorway. By now his jacket and waistcoat had been discarded. His tie was gone and his top button was open, sleeves rolled up. His hair was mussed and stubble lined his jaw.

He looked as if he could step straight into a boxing-ring for a bare-knuckle fight and win.

She put down the plates she'd gathered. 'Um…okay.'

'Our plans have changed.'

She frowned. '*Our* plans?'

'That man—the older gentleman?'

Ashling nodded. She'd chatted to him throughout the day when they'd taken breaks between meetings. A charming man and the only one to acknowledge her. She'd gone out of her way to make sure he had everything he needed.

'Well, I don't know if you know this, but he was the guest of honour today. The man I came to meet. All the other people were members of his and my legal teams. We're working on a top-secret deal together—hence meeting in Paris. His name is Georgios Stephanides. He owns a bank in Greece—one of the most respected in the world.'

'Oh, wow. He seemed so…unassuming.'

'He liked you. What did you do to him? Did you recognise him?'

Ashling looked at Zach and put her hands on her hips, indignant. '*Do* to him? Of course I didn't "do" anything to him, or recognise him. I wouldn't know one end of a banker from the other!'

'Yet he kept seeking you out.' Suspicion rang in Zach's tone.

Not liking how his distrust made her feel, Ashling said, 'When he arrived he dropped his papers and he looked a little shaken. I helped him—got him water… chatted to him. That was all. I had no idea who he was.'

Zach looked unconvinced. 'He wants us to go to dinner with him and his wife this evening, and the deal is too important for me to refuse.'

Ashling squeaked, '*Us?* But there is no…"us". He knows I'm just a temporary assistant.'

'Well, he's invited you too, so we're staying for the night. We'll go to my apartment now, to get ready—it's not far.'

Ashling's insides plummeted. 'But I've nothing with me.'

'My housekeeper keeps the guest suite stocked for such emergencies. I'm sure you'll find something suitable to wear.'

Zach was already turning and walking out of the room, assuming she was right behind him.

Ashling felt like stamping her foot. Instead she called after him, 'I could have plans for this evening, you know.'

He turned around. 'Do you?'

'Well…no,' she admitted reluctantly. 'But I could.'

'But you don't. We don't have much time. My driver is waiting.'

Ashling really had no choice. She could make a fuss and insist on getting the train back to London—assuming there even was one this evening. Or she could just suck this up, and hopefully Zachary Temple would be so sick of the sight of her by tomorrow that he'd consider her debt paid and she wouldn't have to see him again.

She longed to call or text Cassie, who would roll her eyes at the latest drama Ashling had become entangled in. But of course she couldn't. Because a) it sounded as if Cassie was entangled in a drama of her own, and b) her friend must never know that this particular crisis involved her boss, Zachary Temple.

Nor could she confide in her the fact that Zach evoked so many things inside her. Guilt, shame, desire…and something far more ambiguous and dangerous. A kind of yearning for him not to look at her as if she was about to put the family silver in her pockets.

He appeared at the door again, pulling on his jacket. 'Ready?'

Ashling just nodded and followed him out of the suite.

Zach's Paris apartment was at the top of one of Paris's typically elegant nineteenth-century buildings, with views no less impressive than from the suite in the hotel. The Eiffel Tower was visible from the main spacious living area.

The décor was understated and luxurious. Modern art mixed with more traditional art on the walls, showing a quirkier side to Zach than Ashling might have expected for someone so…serious.

A middle-aged lady had met them at the door. Zach had introduced her as Cécile, and she came to Ashling now, saying in accented English, 'Please, follow me, Miss Doyle. I'll show you to your room and where the clothes are.'

Ashling followed her. Zach had disappeared—presumably to his own suite—to get ready.

Ashling's jaw dropped when she walked in. The room was massive, with a huge bed in the centre. There was a terrace outside. The bathroom was sleek in black and white, with a massive modern shower and a tub big enough for more than one person. Her cheeks grew warm.

Then there was the dressing room...

Cécile pointed to some hanging dresses. 'I'm sure there will be something in your size, Miss Doyle. You will find everything you need—including fresh underwear, nightclothes, shoes and accessories. There are new toiletries in the bathroom. '

Ashling was stunned. She asked faintly, 'Does Mr Temple have many overnight guests?'

The woman smiled enigmatically. 'Mr Temple likes to be prepared for every eventuality. This is simply a courtesy for guests.'

The woman left Ashling and she revolved in a circle slowly, taking in the sheer opulence. All the dresses had tags on, so they'd never been worn. As if a man like Zachary Temple would be crass enough to reuse his lovers' dresses! Not that she was a lover... She was just a thorn in his side and he'd decided to torture her a little.

After taking a quick shower and drying her hair, Ashling put on a voluminous robe and went back into the dressing room. A shimmer of dark blue silk caught her eye and she reached in to pull out a dress looked as if it was knee-length which should be suitable for dinner.

Ashling took off the robe and slipped the dress on over brand new underwear. Sleeveless, it had a Grecian design, with a deep vee at the front and velvet bands just under her breasts. It fell to just below her knee in luxurious folds, with a slit to one side. It was simple and effortlessly elegant in the way that only designer clothes could be.

She found a pair of silver high-heeled sandals in her size, and a black clutch bag.

She did the best she could with her hair, taming it into sleek waves, tucked behind one ear and loose on the other side. There was a selection of unused make-up in the bathroom, so she aimed for a slightly dramatic look with an eye pencil, mascara and some cream blusher, a nude lipstick.

She checked her reflection one last time and, conscious that Zach would probably already be waiting, went to the door and opened it—and came to a startled halt when her vision was filled with a naked chest.

Zach's naked chest, specifically. Because he was indeed changing into his tuxedo in his own suite, which must adjoin this guest one—a detail that Ashling registered only very vaguely in that moment.

She'd never seen a naked male torso like it up close. Naturally bronzed skin over taut muscles…a sprinkling of dark hair covering his pectorals and then descending in a dark line, bisecting the ridges of muscle on either side of his hard abdomen before disappearing under the belt and waistband of the trousers sitting on slim hips.

There was not an ounce of excess flesh. He had the body of an elite athlete. Or a warrior.

She didn't even realise she was ogling until Zach cleared his throat and said, 'Lost, Ashling?'

She looked up, not able to stop her cheeks flaming. 'Sorry... I... I didn't realise the rooms were connected...the wrong door...'

He was shrugging on a pristine white shirt now, doing up the buttons, and still she felt as if she was stuck in quick-drying cement. Somehow she managed to make her limbs move, and she turned around just as Zach said, 'You found a dress, I see?'

She stopped on the threshold and turned again slowly, breathing in a sigh of both relief and regret that his shirt was now closed.

'Yes, thank you. I hope it's suitable. I'm not sure what the dress code is...'

His dark gaze felt very clinical as it moved over her. 'It's perfect. You can wait for me in the reception room. I'll be there shortly.'

Ashling turned again and fled, closing the door firmly behind her. No doubt he'd suspect that she'd done that on purpose.

When they emerged from the building a short while later, onto the street, a young man got out of a sleek low-slung silver car and threw the key to Zach, who caught it deftly. He went over and opened the passenger door.

Ashling was too stunned to move. Faintly, she said, 'That's an Aston Martin.'

'Yes, it is.'

For a blessed moment Zach was eclipsed. Ashling

walked over and touched the car reverently, skimming its sinuous lines with her hand. She couldn't *not* touch it.

Zach asked, 'You know about cars?'

She looked at him, aghast. 'This is more than a mere car.'

His mouth quirked. 'I'd have to agree with that.'

She turned back to the car and shook her head. 'I've never seen one up close before.'

'We should get going.'

Zach stood by the passenger door and Ashling got in as gracefully as she could manage. The door closed, sealing her inside possibly the most luxurious and expensive confined space she'd ever been in in her life.

She breathed in with appreciation, unaware of the bemused look Zach sent her as he got into the driver's seat and started the engine.

When he'd pulled away from the kerb and into the early-evening Paris traffic, he glanced at her. 'So how did the interest in cars come about?'

'Because I'm a girl, and girls shouldn't be interested in things like cars?'

Zach was unrepentant. 'It's not that common.'

'No,' she conceded, 'I guess not. I went through a phase when I was younger. I was obsessed with cars and driving. A man we lived with taught me to drive and I got my licence. I haven't driven in a while, though, as there's no real need in London.'

'It wasn't your father who taught you?'

Ashling tensed. She had let that slip out. 'No. I didn't grow up with my father. My parents broke up soon after I was born.'

To her relief Zach didn't ask her about that. He just said, 'So, the man who taught you to drive...?'

Ashling let the tactile contours of the seat mould around her. 'He lived at the commune. He used to be a racing car driver but he got injured.'

'The *commune*?'

Ashling's mouth quirked at the tone in his voice. She glanced at him. They were stopped at a traffic light. He arched a brow, waiting for elaboration. The surreal feeling of being in this legendary car with this man, about to go around the even more iconic Arc de Triomphe, was almost too much for her to process. It made it relatively easy to tell him her colourful background story.

Zach moved smoothly with the traffic as Ashling explained.

'My mum stopped working for Cassie's father when Cassie went to boarding school. We went back to Ireland, where she's from. She had friends living in an artists' commune in the west of Ireland, so we went there.'

'I thought I detected an accent.' Zach noted.

Ashling wrinkled her nose. 'I only spent a few years in Ireland, really, before coming back to London. And "commune" makes it sounds like something from the sixties, when really it was just a kind of collective, where we all pitched in and shared and bartered goods. We grew our own vegetables. Had chickens. It's called an eco-village now. She still lives there, with her new partner Eamon. He's a sheep-farmer and a traditional Irish musician.'

'Your mother sounds...unconventional.'

Ashling hated that word. It was the word her father had used in order to dump her and her mother. Ashling's mother had been too *unconventional* for him, a successful businessman. And yet her unconventionality had been what had drawn him to her in the first place.

She pushed aside old pain and memories of her mother, hurt and diminished by rejection. Thankfully she'd moved on from that now.

A man like Zach, who came from a privileged world, would never understand the life they'd lived. That reminder of who he was made her feel disappointed and defensive all at once. And angry with herself for her helpless attraction to him.

She forced a breezy nonchalance into her voice, hiding the much stronger emotions he'd precipitated. 'Yes, my mother was unconventional, but she was also kind and loving and nurturing. I never lacked for anything. She went back to college and got a master's in Psychotherapy, and now she runs her own practice. She's amazing.'

She felt Zach glance at her. 'I didn't mean it as a criticism. Taking you to Paris for your eighteenth birthday was a pretty special thing to do.'

Ashling forced herself to relax. He couldn't know he pushed her buttons just by being...himself. 'Yes, it was.'

'Did you miss having a father?'

The question surprised Ashling. She wouldn't have expected Zach to want to pursue a personal conversation.

The sky was darkening to violet outside, heightening the sense of being in a luxurious cocoon and Ashling hesitated, thinking of all the moments when she'd seen other kids interact with their fathers and had felt that sharp pang of envy. It was one of the reasons she'd bonded so quickly with Cassie—because while Cassie's father was alive, she'd lost her mother at a young age, so they'd shared the loss of a parent on either side.

Ashling's mother had become a sort of surrogate mother to Cassie. As for Cassie's father, though, he hadn't approved of Ashling and Cassie's friendship, never missing an opportunity to remind Ashling of her rightful place.

'I can't say I didn't, because of course I did, but I wouldn't swap the upbringing I had for the world. My mother made sure I felt loved and secure in a way that most kids with two parents don't get.' She made a small face, unable to stop herself from admitting, 'That's to say that while I don't regret anything, if I had a choice I'd probably choose a more…settled life for my own family. I was always a little envious of Cassie that she had a home that didn't change and move every few years.'

'So you want a family some day?'

Ashling blanched. She'd already said too much. No way was she divulging her deeply secret daydreams of a gaggle of children who would be siblings to each other, because she'd always felt that lack in her own life.

She felt Zach glance at her and kept her answer vague? 'Well, I guess so—doesn't everyone? Don't you?' she tacked on hurriedly, hoping to deflect his attention from her.

She looked at him. If she hadn't, she might have missed the clenching of his jaw before it relaxed again.

He said, 'I expect I'll have a family one day.'

With the kind of woman Ashling had seen him with

four years ago. Patrician. Beautiful. With the right bloodline.

Curious, she said, 'You don't sound too enthusiastic about it.'

He made a little shrugging movement. 'Family is about legacy and continuity.'

The faintly hollow tone in his voice made her wonder what his family was like. She imagined similarly stern parents. Nannies doing the grunt work of parenting. Boarding school? Ashling felt a pang, thinking of a young, dark-haired boy being left at the gates of a Gothic mansion. Then she cursed herself for letting her imagination run away with itself.

She said, 'For someone like you, I can see that legacy and continuity would be important. After all, what would I have to pass on to the next generation?'

Zach slid her a glance. 'A talent for amateur dramatics and causing trouble?'

CHAPTER FIVE

THEY WERE WALKING into the restaurant and Zach should have had his mind on the dinner ahead—it was a good sign that Georgios Stephanides wanted to get to know him better—but he was still thinking about the fact that he'd unwittingly brought up the subject of family with Ashling, when it was something he preferred to avoid thinking about at all costs.

The very notion of family was toxic to him. And yet he'd made a promise to his mother that he would not let the Temple name die out. That he would do her sacrifices justice by creating his own legacy. By having a family.

And, worse than that, he was distracted by Ashling's reaction to his last flippant comment about amateur dramatics. He didn't like the way it had affected his conscience.

She'd looked at him with an expression of hurt and something else on her face before she'd quickly hidden it. It reminded him uncomfortably of how she'd looked at him that night four years ago, when he'd told her he wouldn't touch a woman like her. She'd looked stricken.

Then she'd said quietly, 'I've told you I'm sorry for what happened that night. I've never done anything like that since then. I knew it was wrong. I couldn't even keep the money they paid me. I'm really not some... opportunistic con artist, but I don't know how to convince you of that if you won't give me a chance.'

The maître d' was approaching them now, an unctuous smile on his face, and Zach took Ashling's arm. She felt very slight next to him. Delicate.

He said, 'Look at me, Ashling.'

He saw the way her jaw tensed, but finally she looked up, blue eyes huge. Her mouth was set. He wanted to see it soften. Wanted to feel it under his again, yielding...

'I'll give you a chance, okay?'

Something flared in her eyes. Her cheeks pinkened. It had a direct effect on his blood, heating it at the most inappropriate moment. He gritted his jaw.

Her mouth softened. 'Thank you, I appreciate it.'

The maître d' reached them and Zach turned his attention to the man—anything to erase that image of Ashling's soft mouth from his brain before he had to sit down and be civilised.

'So you don't work for Zach full time, then, no?'

Ashling shook her head at the very glamorous wife of Georgios Stephanides. Elena had short silver hair and beautiful features, and she was as genial as her husband.

'No. My best friend Cassie is Mr...er... Zach's executive assistant. She's in the States for a couple of weeks, and Cassie's own assistant is out sick, so Zach needed help at the last minute.'

Or, more accurately, needed vengeance.

The older woman's dark eyes were as shrewd as

her husband's. She looked from Ashling to Zach, who was deep in conversation with her husband, and then she said, 'So tell me, dear, what do you normally do?'

Ashling smiled, glad of the change of subject away from Zach and her role. 'I'm a yoga teacher, mainly, but I dabble in a few other things as well.'

The woman's face lit up. 'Yoga saved my life after I had a back operation. Now, tell me which kind you practice…'

'They're a lovely couple.'

Zach looked at Ashling. Her skin was lustrous in the dim light of the car. 'That's one way of putting it. You do realise that Stephanides is one of the most power- ful men in Europe, if not the world?'

Ashling shrugged. 'I don't care about any of that. He's down to earth. Nice. They both are.'

Zach made a sound. He'd seen Georgios Stepha- nides's less genial side. But he had to admit that Ash- ling was right. Georgios was no push-over, but he was a rare thing: a humble billionaire.

'So what's the deal you're working on? Or is it too top secret to divulge?'

Every instinct within Zach screamed at him not to say a word. After all, that was how he'd achieved the success he had. By trusting no one. It was lesson he'd learnt at an early age, when he'd tried to make friends at a new school. A boarding school in the middle of nowhere. He'd been twelve years old.

They hadn't been interested in making friends though. Only giving him a lesson in knowing his place. They'd given him a bloody nose and then sneered at him. 'Listen up, Temple. You are not one of us and you never will be, so let's not pretend otherwise, hmm? You're only here because you're a box-ticking exercise in showing charity to the underprivileged. No matter where you end up, you'll never be one of us.'

One of the boys had punctuated that speech by spitting on him where he'd lain on the ground. That had been Zach's first lesson in learning control. Stopping himself from going after them and punching and kicking until the humiliation went away.

And then—many years later—this very woman beside him, in a cheap red wig and a tarty dress, had given him a refresher lesson in not letting his guard drop. Ever.

Now she cut into the slew of unwelcome memories, saying quickly, 'Actually, of course you can't say anything.'

But, perversely, in spite of the memories and his better instincts, Zach felt a strong compulsion to speak. Before he could overthink it, he was saying, 'Georgios and his wife never had children. So he's looking for someone who can take the reins of his bank. He wants to retire and move into philanthropy.'

Ashling looked at him, compassion all over her face. 'Oh, no, that's awful. Elena never mentioned anything…they would have made great parents too.'

Zach had never considered that, because his own view of family was so ambivalent. It was slightly jarring to think of his business acquaintance as someone who might have felt the lack of a family.

And he noted uncomfortably that Ashling's first reaction hadn't been to comment on the fact that he'd just revealed he was in line to take over one of the world's oldest and most respected financial institutions.

Feeling a little bemused, Zach said, 'Elena seemed to like you.'

'Not everyone has the worst impression of me. She's interested in yoga—we talked about that.'

He had to admit—reluctantly—that Ashling had been a good foil this evening. Easy company. He thought of the hurt look on her face when he'd made that comment about amateur dramatics.

Maybe he was being unfair to judge her wholly based on one incident four years ago. She was either telling the truth about it being a one-off, and she really was just a scatty friend of Cassie's. Or she was lying through her teeth and still angling to make the most of this opportunity.

Had she really grown up on a commune with a mother who sounded like the ultimate hippy? He felt something reckless move through him. He wanted her to prove that he was wrong to give her a chance. That she wasn't innocent of trying to seduce him in his own home.

On the spur of the moment Zach pulled in at the side of the road.

She looked at him. 'What are you doing?'

He got out of the car and went around to open Ashling's door.

He said, 'Do you want to have a go?'

She looked up at him, comprehension dawning on her face. 'You mean the car? Drive the car?'

He shrugged. 'Sure—why not? I'm not precious about things like that.'

'But...but I haven't driven in a while. It's an Aston Martin!' she spluttered.

'You know how to drive, don't you?'

'Yes, but this is the other side of the road. I mean, it's not even a road—it's the Champs-élysées!'

'It's just a road. My apartment isn't far from here. I'll direct you.'

A mixture of excitement and shock warred on Ashling's expressive face.

He half expected her to confess that she didn't actually know how to drive, but then she scrambled out of the car, the slit in the dress showing one very taut and toned thigh.

She was breathless. 'Okay, I'll give it a go.'

Zach realised that what he was doing was madness. They were on one of the world's most famous roads. If anything happened it would be splashed all over the papers. But that uncustomary reckless spirit moved through him again.

He watched Ashling walk around and get into the driver's seat. He got into the car.

Ashling wondered if she was having an out-of-body experience. She felt the steering wheel under her hands, the leather warm from Zach's touch. Looked at the lit-up dashboard with its iconic design. Heard the low, throaty purr of the engine.

It was automatic, so she didn't have to worry about the gearstick, and Zach pointed out a few things. When there was a lull in the traffic, she followed Zach's instructions to move out into the road, the car throbbing with barely leashed power underneath her. To her intense embarrassment it made her think of Zach and how he might feel if he was under her...

'Red light,' Zach said.

Ashling pulled to a smooth stop, breathing deep

to try and calm her racing heart. Awe and excitement flooded her blood. 'It feels amazing. So light, but powerful at the same time.'

'I wanted an Aston Martin ever since I saw my first Bond movie as a kid.'

Ashling hit the accelerator again when the light went green. The car surged forward with the barest tap. When she felt she had it under control, she sneaked a quick glance at Zach. 'You were a Bond fan?'

'Still am.'

'I loved them too,' she admitted. 'Even though my mother could never understand my obsession. I think it was the cars and gadgets I loved more than anything else.'

'Not the wealth? The glamour?'

Ashling was barely aware of Zach's question as she concentrated on not crashing the car. 'No, I was never into those things. My favourite gadget was the rocket belt Sean Connery wore in *Thunderball*.'

'Take the next left.'

Ashling was both relieved and disappointed to see the concierge step out of Zach's building onto the quiet street as she came to a stop outside. She was still reeling from the shock of him letting her do this.

She looked at Zach, feeling shy. 'Thank you. This was…amazing.'

'You're a good driver. Next time we should go somewhere you can really let her run.'

Ashling blanched a little. *Next time?*

As if he'd just realised what he'd said, Zach's face shuttered. He got out of the car and came around to help her out. The concierge took care of parking the car. Ashling told herself that what Zach had just said was a slip of the tongue. He obviously didn't mean it.

In the lift on the way up, she studiously avoided looking at him. There was tension in the air, though, something hot and restless.

When the doors opened he let her step out first. She turned around and a wave of gratitude for the experience he'd just given her made her act on impulse. She stepped forward and reached up, pressing a kiss to his jaw in almost exactly the same spot she'd kissed him that night four years ago.

His scent hit her, hurtling her back in time. She regretted it as soon as it had happened. She stepped back, her face flaming. His was unreadable. *Oh, God.* He'd think she was trying to seduce him again.

'Sorry, I just… I didn't mean to do that. I just wanted to say thanks…that was an amazing thing to do… I'm quite tired now. I'll go to bed. Night, Zach.'

And she fled.

Zach watched Ashling disappear. Almost absently he touched his jaw, as if expecting to feel some kind of a mark. She'd barely pressed her lips there, but it burned.

Cursing himself, and the reckless urge that he'd given in to—the same urge that now made him want to follow her to her room and crush her mouth under his, punish her for appearing in his life again and for making him want her—Zach turned and went into the reception room.

It was vast and silent. He stopped on the threshold, struck by that fact. He'd never really noticed it before, but he realised now that he usually didn't let the silence in.

For his whole life he'd been alone to a lesser or greater extent. An only child. And then, at school, once his aptitude had become apparent, he'd been put under a punishing regime by his mother to succeed at all costs. There'd been no room for friends. For frivolous pursuits.

He'd soon learnt to stay apart. Not only to focus, but also because he knew he wasn't welcome. It had become like a second skin—the fact that he didn't need anyone else. And if he had ever felt the lack he'd shut it out with work. Or, later, with sex.

But here, now, after Ashling's disappearance, he could feel the void. The absence of her bright presence. She had an effervescence that drew people to her. He'd seen it in the way Georgios and his wife had reacted to her.

The fact that Ashling tapped into Zach's sense of isolation wasn't welcome. Was that what had prompted him to suggest another outing in the car before he'd even realised what he was saying? He was usually so careful around women, never putting himself in any position that might lead them to think he wanted more than a finite affair.

Zach heard a noise behind him and turned around.

Ashling was standing in the doorway. Barefoot.

The introspection of moments before dissolved in her presence. He instantly felt warmer. *Less isolated.*

She looked hesitant. 'I just… I just wanted to say I really hope you don't think that when I kissed you just now it was because I was trying to do anything…because I really wasn't. And last night too. I wasn't trying to seduce you.' She gave a little laugh that sounded strained. 'I've had two boyfriends and neither lasted very long. I'm really not that...experienced.'

Her face went crimson. She half turned away.

Zach heard her say, almost to herself, 'I can't believe I just said that...' She looked back. 'Forget I said anything. I'll leave you—'

'Don't.'

Zach knew he should resist, but in actuality he couldn't. He needed something from her in that moment. Something he'd never needed from another woman because no other woman had impacted him the way she did. *Connection*.

The sharp tone of Zach's voice stopped Ashling in her tracks. She looked at him. He dominated the vast space around him. The Eiffel Tower glittered like a bauble through the window behind him.

Ashling forced her voice to work. 'Don't...what?'

'Don't leave.' His voice sounded rough.

Ashling's heart hitched. Her skin prickled all over. The air was thick. Heavy with a tension she could feel coiling tight in her lower body.

Zach walked towards her, shucking off his jacket as he did so, dropping it on a chair. He stopped a few inches away, his gaze roving over her face.

He said, 'I gave you the impression last night that I didn't want you. But that wasn't entirely fair. And neither was what I said four years ago—that you were the last woman I would touch. You made an impression on me. That's why I recognised you. I never forgot your face. The truth is from the moment I saw you, I wanted you.'

Ashling swallowed. *He did fancy her.* It was too much to absorb for a second.

'The woman you were with that night...'

'She dumped me—like I told you. But I didn't care. I was angry at first, but then I realised that I didn't even want her any more.'

Because he'd wanted her...?

Ashling shook her head. 'You're just saying this. Teasing me. More punishment for what I did.'

She turned to go but Zach caught her hand, lacing his fingers through hers. It felt shockingly intimate.

'I'm not teasing. I don't tease women. It tends to send out the wrong message.'

Ashling could believe that. He was far too serious. She wondered what he would be like if he laughed. Properly laughed. Out loud. Smiled.

'So what...?' *What happens now?* She couldn't say the words out loud.

Zach tugged her closer. He lifted their entwined hands against his chest and curled his other hand around her neck. Just before his mouth descended on hers, Ashling realised he wasn't asking her permission because she'd made it all too painfully obvious that she wanted him. For a second she wanted to pull back, disconcert him as he did her, so easily, but then his mouth touched hers and the world went on fire.

Ashling could feel the press of Zach's arousal against her belly. She strained closer, seeking friction to assuage the ache building between her legs, sharp and urgent.

Zach pushed the strap of her dress off one shoulder. He untwined his fingers from hers and Ashling's hand slid over his chest, revelling in the sheer breadth and

strength of him. He was tugging her head back, deep-
ening the kiss, drugging her, pulling her deeper and
deeper into a carnal spell where the whole world, her
very existence, was reduced to this moment, with her
heart beating and the delicious tug and pull of Zach's
tongue against hers.

And then he broke the kiss, trailing his mouth down
over her shoulder. She realised through a hot haze that
he was resting back on the arm of a couch and had
spread his legs either side of her thighs, so that he
could trap here there. It placed his erection closer to
the apex of her legs, and Ashling bit her tongue at the
sharp tug of need.

He pulled down the strap of the dress further, until
one side of her dress was peeled away from her bare
breast. He looked up at her for a moment, dark eyes
hooded and full of something that made her shake.
She'd never known she could have such an effect on a
man. Or a man on her. Her previous experiences hadn't
prepared her remotely for this rush of sensations and
desires piling up inside her, stealing her sanity and
her wits and—

Ashling let out a low moan when Zach's mouth surrounded the peak of her breast in hot, sucking heat.

Her hands clasped his head. She was torn between
pulling him back from torturing her and keeping him
there for ever. He laved the hard peak with his tongue,
teeth nipping gently, before sucking so hard that Ashling saw stars. She didn't even know if she was still
standing. Every nerve cell was straining towards a release that shimmered just out of reach...

And then his other hand was under her dress, reaching up to find her thigh, caressing her there, moving

higher, fingers sliding under silk underwear to cup her bottom.

Ashling couldn't think or breathe, but something was struggling to reach her through the fog. A small voice. A warning. She didn't really know this man. He was Cassie's *boss*! She'd done something awful to him in the past and he hated her for it. So how could he now—?

Ashling tensed and pushed back, dislodging Zach's mouth from her breast. She pulled the dress back up over her throbbing breast, securing the strap on her shoulder again with shaking fingers. Her blood was pounding. Her body crying out for fulfilment.

But she wasn't even sure if she liked this man, and yet he'd connected with her on a level so deep and intimate that it made her head spin.

She took a step back and said shakily, 'I don't think this is a good idea. You're Cassie's boss. She's my friend. You don't even like me. You don't trust me.'

Zach's hair was mussed. *She'd done that, grabbing his head to keep his mouth on her breast.* She could still feel the delicious tugging—

She closed her eyes in a bid to stop her imagination.

'I don't trust anyone.'

Ashling's eyes snapped open again. Zach stood up and went over to a drinks cabinet. He poured himself a measure of golden liquid, asked, 'Do you want a drink?'

Ashling shook her head. Then said, 'No, thank you.'

I don't trust anyone.

He looked very remote at that moment, his back to her. Ashling wanted to go and put her arms around him from behind, press close. The men she'd been with before—sweet and kind and ultimately dull—would have let her do that. But this man…he would resist. And the fact that she knew that and yet still wanted to do it told her she was doing the right thing.

Zachary Temple was not looking for comfort. He was not even someone she thought she could admire. He shouldn't be having this effect on her. It made her wonder about the rock-solid values she'd taken for granted her whole life, having been taught that things like compassion, wellbeing, happiness and good health were more important than wealth and ambition.

This just proved to Ashling that passion was dangerous. It scrambled your brain cells. Made you fall for the wrong person. Made you trust in something that wasn't there. Like her mother and her father.

Something struck her. Maybe the men she'd been with before had been attractive to her precisely because she'd known they wouldn't push her to the edge of her boundaries and over. It wasn't a welcome revelation.

She wondered if she really knew herself at all. How could someone like Zach fascinate her so much when he'd just been handed everything his whole life? When he was so ambitious—pursuing a deal to gain control of one of Europe's biggest banks just to add it to his portfolio?

She backed away to the door even as her body still ached for satisfaction. 'This isn't a good idea. I'll go.'

Zach didn't turn around. He just took a swig of the drink and said, 'That's probably a good idea.'

Ashling turned and left on very shaky limbs. It was as if an earthquake had just exploded inside her and her cells had been rearranged. She knew that on some fundamental level Zach had triggered a response that she would never be able to bury or deny again. He'd changed her, whether she liked to admit it or not. In spite of who he was.

Zach knew that no amount of alcohol burning its way down his throat would extinguish the desire that had just knocked him off his feet. He'd felt it last night, but he'd not given it full rein. Just now, though…it had almost overwhelmed him. The feel of Ashling's mouth under his…her tongue shyly touching his…her slender limbs that belied the strength he'd felt in her muscles… soft breasts, filling his hand and his mouth.

No woman had ever made him lose it. He'd seen his peers fall by the wayside, seemingly driven mad with lust they couldn't control…he'd pitied them.

But just now he'd been afraid to turn around in case Ashling saw the extent of the need still burning him up inside written all over his face. He felt feral. Animalistic.

He should be secretly thankful that she'd pulled them back from the brink. She was right. They shouldn't be doing this—for many reasons. Not least of which was because she was not his type at all. And he suspected she'd tell him that he wasn't hers.

But instead of feeling thankful, all he felt was seriously unsatisfied. And angry with himself for his serious lapse in judgement. He'd shared top secret information with her, and now he had to face the prospect that letting her go was not an option.

The following morning Ashling felt heavy-headed after a restless night. She'd been too keyed-up to sleep. Too full of aches and wants.

Zach, on the other hand, when she met him in the dining room for breakfast, looked as pristine as if he'd just spent a weekend at a spa resort. Clean-shaven. Hair damp from a shower. Smelling delicious. The worst thing was that she could imagine only too well the power behind his civilised clothes. The warm silky skin over steel muscles.

He looked at her when she sat down at the table, not a hint of what had happened the previous evening in his expression or his eyes. It was disconcerting.

But then Ashling had to remind herself that Zach was far more used to this kind of thing than she was. And in a way she should be thankful they hadn't slept together, because there was no way she knew how to navigate a morning-after situation with a man like him.

He poured her a cup of coffee. There were delicious-looking pastries and fluffy croissants laid out on trays.

'What are your plans this week?' he asked.

Ashling picked up the cup, hoping the coffee might make her feel half as put-together as he looked.

She stared at him. 'Plans?'

He nodded.

Feeling a little nonplussed, Ashling said, 'I have yoga classes to teach, and I care for Mrs Whyte—'

'Mrs Whyte?'

'The woman whose shopping I buy. I delivered it to her yesterday…when you came to my apartment?'

Zach nodded. 'Yes, go on, what else?'

Ashling put down the cup. 'Apart from the yoga and Mrs Whyte I have a couple of shifts at the cafe… I think that's it. Why?'

'I need you to work for me this week.'

'You…what?'

'I'm still without assistants. Gwen will be out for another week at least. Cassie isn't due back until the end of the week after next. And Georgios Stephanides wants to move ahead with this deal. I'm hosting an event at my Somerset house at the end of next week and he's coming with his wife to talk over final details. I've told you this deal is top secret. I don't want anyone else to know what's going on until contracts are signed. You and my legal team are the only ones in the loop. And Georgios has met you. He thinks you're part of my team. He likes you. He sent a message this morning saying that he hoped you'd be there, which is as good as an order.'

'But you don't trust me.'

Because he didn't trust anyone.

Had her actions four years ago had this effect on his outlook? Ashling told herself she was being ridiculous. She might have caused him some embarrassment, but she'd hardly have enough influence to cause him to become less trusting. He moved in a world where cynicism pervaded everything.

Zach countered with, 'Precisely. Not only do I need to keep Georgios Stephanides happy, I also want you where I can see you.'

Ashling chafed at that. 'I'm not a child.'

Something flared in his eyes. 'No, you're not...'

Ashling flushed. 'I can't just drop everything at the last minute. What I do might not seem consequential to you, but I can assure you that—'

'I'm sure your neighbour would appreciate full-time care, no?'

Ashling's mouth stayed open. 'What are you saying?'

'That if you work for me for the week I'll ensure that she has help for as long as she needs it.'

Ashling struggled to take this in. 'But that's...that's like winning the lottery.'

Zach shrugged minutely.

Anger at his cavalier attitude to something potentially life-changing flared up inside Ashling. 'People are just pawns to you, aren't they? You're angry with me so you've moved me around to teach me a lesson. And now you think you can just click your fingers and change someone's life just because it's expedient for *you*.'

'I don't let things stand in my way.'

'Because you don't have to.'

'Because I've worked for it.'

'I doubt that,' she scoffed. 'Someone like you was born with a golden ticket into the arena.'

Zach's face tightened. 'You know this because...?'

A prickle of unease skated down Ashling's spine. 'Because it's obvious.'

Was it, though? a little voice prompted. It wasn't like her to judge. But Zach oozed privilege. To get to his level of success demanded entry at the very top levels of society from birth. She pushed aside her conscience.

'You'd really set up care for Mrs Whyte for as long as she needs it?'

'Consider it done.'

'I'd have to talk to her...see if it's something she wants. She's very private.'

'I can offer her more consistent care than you ever could. With the best will in the world.'

That stung. But Ashling knew it was true. She

couldn't guarantee that she'd always be there, and Mrs Whyte had grown quite dependent on her.

Zach said, 'You still owe me, Ashling. There is a deal here that I want very badly. If you can help me close it then we really will be quits.'

Ashling squirmed inwardly at the thought of causing him to lose a deal four years before. The guilt was still fresh. 'I'd have to sort out my other commitments. My yoga classes. The café.''

'Whatever you need to do—do it.'

In other words this was a fait accompli and Ashling was being sucked into Zach's orbit whether she liked it or not.

Much to her disgust, her prevailing reaction was one of illicit excitement, not outright rejection of this turn of events. And, even worse, she realised that her anger had flared so quickly not just because of his arrogance in knowing that he would prevail no matter what, but because just a few hours ago she'd been a very willing pawn in his arms.

Nevertheless, she forced herself to say, 'What about…what happened last night?'

Zach's jaw clenched. 'That was a mistake. It won't happen again.'

CHAPTER SIX

ZACH BLINKED. LESS than twenty-four hours later, Ashling stood in the doorway to his office wearing a blue silk sleeveless jumpsuit. A yellow belt cinched her waist and a yellow neckerchief adorned her throat. She wore yellow wedge sandals. A jaunty cross-over pink bag rested at her hip.

She looked bright and fresh. And totally out of place. And yet something perverse inside him made him resist his reflex to instruct HR to discreetly let her know there was a dress code. After all, this was just a temporary arrangement.

You could have let her go.

He *should* have let her go.

Especially after what had happened the night before last.

Especially because the lust she'd awakened inside him was snapping back to life now.

He ignored his libido and stood up. 'Come in, Ashling.'

She looked nervous and that caught at him. He told himself he was being ridiculous. She was street-smart and savvy.

But she must have seen his look and she said, a little defensively, 'I'm not used to this kind of environment.'

'And you're really not that interested, are you?' Zach noted dryly.

She flushed. Looked behind him. 'The views are amazing.'

Zach rested back on the side of his desk. 'So is the wealth I generate for my clients.'

'You hardly need my approval for that.'

Zach cocked his head. 'You really expect me to believe that wealth, success, means nothing to you?'

'Oh, it means everything—I just measure wealth and success differently.'

'Says the woman who loves an Aston Martin, one of the most expensive cars in the world.'

She flushed again. It was fascinating to watch her react to things.

'I can appreciate a beautiful car without wanting to acquire it as a trophy.'

Zach made a wincing face. 'Ouch.'

Now she looked contrite. 'I'm sorry, that wasn't fair—especially after you let me drive yours.'

Zach stood up, realising he was indulging in exactly the kind of chatter he expressly forbade among his employees. 'I'll have HR send someone up to show you how to navigate the computer system. Essentially, though, your job is just about running interference. They'll explain everything. You can use the desk in the office next door.'

Ashling took a deep breath after she had put a closed door between her and Zach. She'd only realised when she'd got to his office that morning and seen him in a dark grey three-piece suit that everyone in the building was similarly attired in monochrome colours. Even the decor was muted. No doubt to minimise distraction.

No wonder people had given her second and third glances on her way up here. A familiar sensation washed over her—she didn't belong here. But she pushed it aside. She hadn't *asked* to be here after all. She'd been *instructed* to be here.

It was as if the universe had conspired with Zach to leave her no option but to do his bidding. Since she'd seen him last Mrs Whyte had met and approved someone from an agency who would help her until such time that she decided she didn't need it any longer. And Ashling had asked a friend to cover her yoga classes, half hoping there might be a problem. But he'd been delighted at the prospect of extra cash.

Similarly, a friend at the café had jumped at the chance of more shifts because she was saving for her wedding.

So now she was here, her heart still palpitating in her chest.

She had the strong impression that, in spite of Zach's justification for asking her to work for him, he was just doing it for his own amusement…stringing her torture out for a bit longer. He probably had a personal bet on how long she would last, so she resolved right then to do everything in her power to confound his expectations.

Except one thing.

She refused to dress to fit in with the crowd.

Two days later, Ashling was making coffee for Zach, expecting his arrival at any moment. She was not a morning person at the best of times, and the effort it had taken for the past two days to be on time—early, in fact—and bright-eyed and bushy-tailed was not inconsequential. But it had been worth it for the look of sheer surprise on Zach's face the first morning and then, yesterday, his look of disbelief.

The fact that he'd evidently expected her to bail within twenty-four hours only spurred her on. With a little judicious borrowing from Cassie's wardrobe Ashling had managed to pull together something resembling a corporate uniform each day. Albeit her kind of corporate uniform…about as far from monochrome as one could get.

She heard a noise in the outer office and her heart thumped. Zach seemed to have had no problem moving on from the other night—as he'd called it, *a mistake*—but for her it wasn't so easy. The tension she felt in his presence coiled tight inside her now, as she anticipated seeing him.

He appeared in the doorway to little kitchen that led into a private dressing room and bathroom. Ashling handed the cup of coffee over carefully, avoiding looking directly at his face. She didn't want to see the cool appraisal he subjected her to every morning.

But then he said, 'Pink today?'

She forced herself to meet his eyes. 'Is that a problem?'

He took a sip of coffee as that dark gaze drifted down from the pussycat bow at her throat—the pink silky shirt had been an impulse buy on her way home the previous day—to the wide-legged three-quarter-length trousers dotted with a variety of colourful flowers and the blue suede high heels. She had to admit that, even for her, there was a lot going on. But in her defence, bleary-eyed that morning, she'd thought the shoes were black.

He raised his gaze again. By now Ashling's pulse was hectic.

He just said, 'Not a problem at all.'

He was turning away, and then he stopped, turned back. 'By the way, I should have mentioned it before, but we have to go to a function this evening. A garden party.'

'I didn't bring anything to change into.'

Zach gestured with his free hand towards the dressing room. 'Cassie usually leaves a selection of outfits here in case of last-minute events. I'm sure you'll find something. If not, just order in.'

Order in. Like a Chinese takeaway.

Ashling felt slightly hysterical at the thought of appearing in public officially as Zach's assistant. What if someone spoke to her and expected her to say something knowledgeable? In Paris she'd been winging it. And that had been a punishment for her transgression. This was… She wasn't even sure what this was. Only that Zach wasn't done with punishing her and that he stirred up so many things inside her that even if he told her she could walk away right now she wasn't sure she'd want to.

At that moment he appeared in the doorway again, without his coffee. He was holding up an object shaped like an egg. 'What is this?'

'Oh, that's just an aromatherapy oil diffuser.' She gestured to the matching device on her desk. 'Mine is a mixture of sage and peppermint. Sage to clear the energy and peppermint to keep things fresh. Raise the vibration.'

He arched a brow. '"Raise the vibration"? "Clear the energy"?'

She nodded. 'It's quite dense in here—but no wonder, considering the stress of your employees.'

'They're stressed?'

She made a face. 'Not in a bad way…just working hard to keep up with your…er…pace. Yours is bergamot, to stay focused and grounded…' Ashling trailed off, sensing she'd lost him as soon as she'd said *energy*.

He just looked at the diffuser in his hand and then walked back into his office with a bemused expression on his face.

Much later that day, after everyone else had left Temple Corp, Zach was escorting Ashling out of the building, across the carefully landscaped concourse, to where his chauffeur-driven car was waiting.

Ashling was self-conscious in the only suitable dress of Cassie's that she'd been able to find in the dressing room. A deep royal blue colour, it matched her shoes. It was a very simple silk shift dress, with thin straps. It reached to the knee. Or just below, in Ashling's case, as she was shorter than Cassie.

Zach was dressed in a tuxedo, and when Ashling had seen him she'd said in dismay, 'I should be wearing a full-length gown… But all of Cassie's are too long on me.'

He'd looked her over. 'You'll be fine—you'll be there as my guest.'

In other words, Ashling had surmised on their short journey down to ground level, it would be obvious that she wasn't Zach's date. It made her wonder if he'd prefer to be taking a woman who *was* a date. Who he wouldn't have to stop kissing because there was just too much baggage between them...

From what Cassie had told her over the years, Zach was discreet to the point of obsession when it came to his personal life. Rarely did any picture surface on-line of him with a woman, and if it did she was always a perfect foil. Tall, sleek, beautiful... There were no kiss-and-tells.

Ashling's conscience pricked. Had what she'd done to him ended up in the papers? She didn't even know because she'd felt so humiliated and guilty. She hadn't looked.

In the back of the car now, heading for central London, Ashling bit her lip, the urge to know trembling on her tongue. But before she could let it out, Zach spoke.

'You've done well these past few days.'

Ashling looked at him, surprised. She knew after only a few days of observing him that he didn't hand out platitudes or compliments. 'Thank you.'

'You're not as ditsy or flaky as Cassie has suggested over the years. Or as you yourself would have people believe, I think.'

Surprise rendered Ashling speechless. No one had ever really taken the time to look past the persona she projected, of a free spirit pinballing her way through life. She knew she used it as a device to protect herself from deeper scrutiny—something her mother had pointed out when she'd been dissecting everyone around her during her Psychotherapy master's degree. The fact that it appeared as if this man—of all people—could see right through her was very exposing.

Telling herself she was silly to feel exposed—after all, Zach wasn't interested in who she really was—she said lightly, 'Who knew that a career spanning everything from waiting tables to teaching yoga would prepare me for one day working for you?'

Zach frowned. 'You didn't go to university?'

Ashling shook her head and forced down the ingrained reflex of feeling inadequate. It had taken her a long time not to feel insecure about her lack of higher education. Even though Cassie had often said to her, *'Ash, I work with people who have degrees coming out their eyeballs and you're smarter than them.'*

She said, 'I'm a little dyslexic, so I was never very academic. I prefer to learn on the job.'

Something else that distanced her from her father, who couldn't be more different, having come from a solidly middle-class academic background.

Zach looked at her for a long moment and she felt like squirming under that dark unreadable gaze. She said, 'I presume you were top of your class?'

His expression was shuttered. 'Something like that.'

Ashling was intrigued. She wanted to know more. She had to concede that this man she'd dismissed for years as arrogant and snobbish was a lot more complex than she'd expected.

And that was her cue to divert the conversation away from personal topics. 'What do you expect me to do at the event?' she asked.

He looked at her. 'Just stay by my side and be a second set of eyes and ears.'

He turned away again, and Ashling curbed the urge to salute and say, *Aye-aye, sir.*

* * *

The gardens attached to the American Ambassador's residence were beautiful and pristinely ornate. Personally, Ashling preferred something a little wilder. Black-clothed staff moved gracefully between the guests, handing out delicious canapés and vintage champagne. Classical music drifted from a gazebo where a small band were playing.

The man Zach had been talking to walked away and Zach turned to Ashling. 'What did you make of him?'

Thankfully, she'd studied the other man, while also being preoccupied by her surroundings. And Zach. A skill she obviously needed.

'Too desperate for your attention. Fake laugh. Untrustworthy.'

She spoke automatically, without thinking, and nearly choked on her wine when Zach threw back his head and laughed out loud. People turned to look, and a very dangerous warmth bloomed in Ashling's chest.

Zach looked down at her, a smile transforming his face from merely gorgeous to savagely beautiful. He looked younger. She couldn't breathe.

'That's certainly one way of putting it—and very accurate,' he said.

Damn him. He was totally irresistible when his stern facade cracked a little. And when she was the cause.

He gestured for her to follow him further into the crowd. Ashling picked her way carefully behind him in her heels, acutely conscious of the fact that most of the other women were wearing long dresses. Not that she needed more help to feel out of place in a situation like this.

A charity auction was taking place in another part

of the garden, with cheers going up every now and then as someone bid successfully on something spectacular.

When there was a brief lull in the steady stream of gushing people seeking an audience with Zach, Ashling said, 'You're not bidding on any of the lots?'

He looked at her. 'I've already given a healthy donation. I don't need to make a public spectacle of myself.'

Ashling's conscience pricked. As if she needed a reminder... Forgetting all about keeping things impersonal, she blurted out, 'Was it very bad? After that night? I mean, I know you told me you lost a deal, and the woman you were with dumped you...'

He arched a brow. 'That wasn't bad enough?'

Ashling regretted her runaway mouth now. But she'd started... 'Did it get into the papers?'

Zach sighed. 'Yes—but thankfully only the gossip section of a couple of rags. It didn't last beyond a couple of weeks. It was the rumours and word of mouth among my peers that did the most damage. People weren't sure if they could trust me. Which was the intention of the person who initiated the whole thing—to destabilise my success.'

'You know who it was?'

'I do.'

It was said with such finality that Ashling didn't dare probe further. The smile was long gone. He was back to being stern.

Someone else approached them and Ashling cursed inwardly. She wanted to ask why people hadn't trusted him when he came from their world. But he looked about as likely to tell her that as he was to tell her that all was forgiven and he trusted her implicitly.

She kicked herself for having mentioned anything.

This…this truce, or whatever it was between them, wouldn't last long if she kept bringing up the past.

Zach was aware of Ashling beside him, swaying to the music. When he glanced at her she had a dreamy look on her face, which completely threw him off the thread of the very boring conversation going on around him.

Her question about what had happened four years ago had brought back unwelcome reminders of a sense of betrayal that still had the power to sting.

Not hurt.

He had to concede now that no one could sustain this level of acting in order to convince him that she really wasn't interested in this world. She wasn't trying to talk to the A-list celebrities. She wasn't goggle-eyed at the fact that a very recent and popular ex-American President was just yards away, holding court with a rapt crowd.

The dreamy look on her face made him feel something completely alien. *Jealous.* He found himself asking something he'd never have asked another woman, 'What are you thinking about?'

The dreamy look disappeared, to be replaced with a sheepish one. 'Sorry—was I meant to be listening in to your conversation? When I heard you talking about stocks and shares I zoned out.'

Zach shook his head. 'No, it's fine.'

Now she looked embarrassed. 'It's this song…it's one of my favourites.'

Zach hadn't even noticed it. But he heard it now. Slow and jazzy. He could imagine Ashling dancing to it, laughing up at someone. A perverse impulse gripped him and he grabbed her hand, tugging her towards the dance floor set up under a canopy of trees full of twinkling lights. He didn't notice them. All he noticed was how small Ashling's hand felt in his. And how he wanted to snarl at anyone who looked at her.

Usually it gave Zach a kind of detached pleasure to know he was with a woman other men coveted. As if it was confirmation that he was *one of them*. But not this time.

Ashling hissed at him. 'What are you doing?'

Zach stepped onto the dance floor and pulled Ashling into his arms. She was so much smaller than him, but she fitted in a way that reminded him all too vividly of how she'd felt in his arms the other night. His blood sizzled.

She was looking up at him. He raised a brow.

She said, 'I didn't have you down as a dancer.'

He wasn't. Not naturally. But in her quest to furnish him with all the skills he'd need to navigate the upper echelons of society his mother had ensured he'd taken lessons long ago. Not that he needed a lesson to hold this woman close and move around the floor with her. She was as light as a feather. But supple. Strong.

'You think I'm dull? Boring?'

Pink tinged Ashling's cheeks. 'Not dull. Or boring. Just…serious.'

A memory came back into Zach's head. A teacher. One of the nice ones. She'd stopped him one day after class and said, 'You don't have to take everything so seriously, Zach. The world won't fall in if you have some fun.'

But he'd never had the freedom that others had to have fun. To fail.

He shoved aside the memories. 'What do you do to have fun?' he asked her.

Ashling bit her lip and Zach's body tightened with need. He gritted his jaw to curb his response. Next to impossible.

'I read,' Ashling said, 'but quite slowly because of my dyslexia. I like cooking… I practise yoga. I love going out and dancing to loud music—the louder the better. Wild swimming…'

'Wild swimming?'

She wrinkled her nose. 'A fancy way of saying swimming outside. Lakes, rivers, the sea… My favourite is to swim in the Atlantic, off the west coast of Ireland. It's wild and magical.'

How was it that Zach, who literally had everything he could possibly want, was feeling jealous again— this time for a life he'd never even imagined existed?

Ashling felt exposed. And acutely aware of how her body was responding to Zach's. She realised she'd not listed one sophisticated pursuit. She sounded like a teenager.

Desperately wanting to deflect Zach's attention from her, she asked abruptly, 'What do *you* do to relax?'

An image popped into her head of Zach in a heaving nightclub, his eyes focused on her as the music pounded like waves around them. He'd be in a T-shirt and worn jeans…the material clinging to his taut muscles. His hands would reach for her, lifting her so that she could wrap her legs around his waist, and he'd be kissing her so deeply that she'd feel it in the centre of her body—

Zach's voice broke through the fever haze in Ashling's mind. 'I go to the gym. I run. I like good whisky. I have a motorbike…but I can't remember the last time I took it out.'

Now the image of him in worn jeans in a nightclub was replaced by an image of Zach on a motorbike, dressed in worn leathers…a white T-shirt. Stubble on his chin. That brooding look on his face.

Ashling swallowed. 'Maybe you should take it out soon.'

He looked at her, and for a second she thought she saw something wistful in his expression before it disappeared. 'Maybe I will.'

Terrified that Zach would see how much he was affecting her, Ashling muttered something about the bathroom and pulled free of his embrace to leave the dance floor, her limbs shaky with need.

When she returned she expected Zach to be surrounded again, but he stood a little way off to the side of the crowd. Ashling's heart squeezed. He looked very…alone.

And then she castigated herself for being so soft. Zach was not someone who invited sympathy. If he was alone it was because he chose to be—because he was brilliant and ruthless and intolerant of anyone who couldn't keep up with him. And yet she knew it wasn't that simple…

He was far too enigmatic. That was the problem.

As if hearing her thoughts, he turned around in that moment. She picked her way carefully over to him. High heels and grass didn't really mix. When she was about a foot away her heel caught and she pitched forward with a little cry. Landing straight into Zach's arms.

A spark of electricity zinged between them. Ashling's breath stopped. For an infinitesimal moment the possibility that Zach would pull her closer, lower his head, seemed to hang in the air... But even as Ashling made a telling movement towards him he was pushing her back, steadying her.

Her face burned and she was glad they were somewhat in the shadows, which were disguising her humiliation. There might be an attraction between them, but it wasn't so overpowering that Zach couldn't resist it. And it would only be because she was a novelty to someone who came from this world.

Exactly as her mother had been to her father. Until he'd realised that her zest for life and her hippyish tendencies wouldn't fit into his world.

Ashling felt ridiculously vulnerable. She'd talked too much about herself this evening. She was out of her depth in this place where women's faces didn't emote and the men all had cynical sharp edges like Zach.

She avoided his eye, not wanting him to see the conflicting emotions she was feeling right now.

And then he said, 'Ready to go?'

She nodded, feeling a mixture of relief and disappointment.

When they were in the back of Zach's car, Ashling said, 'Your driver can drop me off at the nearest tube.'

'No way. He's driving you home.'

'But I—'

'No arguments. I'd do the same for Cassie.'

That stopped Ashling protesting further. She knew

very well that Zach's driver often dropped Cassie home after-hours.

She was glad her friend wasn't around at the moment. The last thing she needed was to have her be witness to the ridiculous crush she'd developed on her boss. Especially when he was a man she'd judged so vociferously in the past, shamefully driven by her guilt about what she'd done when she'd first met him.

Just as they were turning into his street, Zach said, 'I have to go to Madrid tomorrow for twenty-four hours. I don't need you to come with me.'

For a second all Ashling was aware of was a rushing sound in her head and the plummeting of her stomach. He was letting her go. He'd seen how much she wanted him and it had embarrassed him. He hadn't really needed her to work for him except to humiliate her, and now her humiliation was complete—

'...hold the fort at the office...call me if there's anything urgent. And don't forget to pack a bag, Gerard will pick us up from the office at lunchtime on Thursday.'

Zach had been speaking all the time, but she hadn't heard him. The car had stopped now. He was looking at her.

'What did you say?' she asked.

'The event at my house in Somerset at the weekend. We leave on Thursday. We'll be back on Saturday.'

Ashling had forgotten. The event at which Georgios Stephanides and his wife were to be the guests of honour. The top secret deal. He wasn't letting her go. He was just going to Madrid.

'I... Of course...okay. I'll be ready.'

Zach got out of the car and walked up the steps.

Ashling saw the door open. He disappeared. The car moved off again.

She tried to deny it, but she couldn't. The relief coursing through her blood was humiliatingly heady.

CHAPTER SEVEN

THE FOLLOWING MORNING—early—Zach's plane took off from the small airfield. His sleep last night had been broken by dreams of dancing with a woman. Of how her body felt against his. Lithe and supple and soft and tempting. With a lush mouth that smiled readily. And huge blue eyes that looked at him as if she genuinely wanted to know what was going on in his head and even deeper. Where he kept things hidden.

At first her hair had been blonde in the dream—a familiar blonde bob—but then he'd realised it was a wig when she'd pulled it off to reveal long red hair underneath, and her smile had turned sly and calculating as everyone around them had stopped to look and laugh.

Zach scowled as the ground dropped away beneath him. He'd made a last-minute decision not to bring Ashling with him to Madrid. But maybe it was a wasted opportunity to seduce her and be done with her. Because no woman ever held any allure for him beyond the conquest.

Ashling might appeal to a different side of him, but once he'd had her she would cease to intrigue him. Cease to have the uncanny ability she seemed to have to be able to tap into his psyche in a way that he really didn't appreciate.

Zach thought ahead to the weekend. Ostensibly Ashling was going to be there to keep Georgios Stephanides happy. The man seemed to find Zach more trustworthy with Ashling around.

Whatever... Zach didn't like feeling as if he was depending on anyone else for success, but Ashling owed him a deal at the very least. After the one she'd been instrumental in ruining four years ago, undoing years of hard work.

But the deal had only been part of it. The rest had been ritual humiliation and the erosion of the respect he'd built up.

Ashling wouldn't really have paid off her debt in full until he had her underneath him, begging for mercy.

Anticipation fired along all his nerve-endings and into his blood as he contemplated the weekend ahead. By the time it was over he would have closed the biggest deal of his life to date and Ashling would have paid her debt to him in full.

Two days later, Ashling was delivered to the private airfield where she'd taken the plane with Zach to Paris. Thankfully she saw him before he saw her, so she had a minute to compose herself. He'd stayed in Madrid longer than he'd intended, but an absence of some thirty-six hours had done nothing to inure her to his effect. There was a helicopter a little bit away from where Zach was talking to a man who looked like a pilot in uniform. And then she realised what Zach was wearing and her brain went into meltdown.

Faded jeans and a dark short-sleeved polo shirt.

Aviator sunglasses. Her imaginings of how he would look in faded jeans could never have come close to the reality. The material cupped his buttocks and his thighs with such indecency that it felt voyeuristic just to look at him.

His arms were crossed over his wide chest and his biceps muscles bulged. The car came to a stop and Zach turned around. Ashling instantly felt she'd chosen the wrong outfit to wear—a short, multi-coloured sleeveless sundress and gladiator sandals. Suddenly she longed to be in one of Cassie's structured suits.

The driver opened her door and helped her out. Butterflies zoomed and collided in her gut as she walked towards Zach. She was glad of her own sunglasses. Two could play the game of hiding.

She saw the driver giving her luggage and what must be Zach's to one of the airport staff. The man Zach had been talking to melted away.

'How was Madrid?' she asked.

'Good.'

Ashling couldn't help wondering if he'd been with a woman. There was a faintly smug—*or satisfied?*—air to his demeanour. Maybe he had a lover there. A sultry Spanish siren with the kind of curves Ashling had longed for ever since she'd started developing. Maybe she'd enticed him to stay. Maybe she'd made him laugh. Made him forget to be serious. Made him kiss her as passionately as he'd kissed Ashling.

Ugh. She was pathetic. And, even more disturbingly, she was *jealous*. Sure now that he must have been with a woman, and that he was probably laughing at her, Ashling all but stomped towards the small private jet.

No man had made her jealous before. Not even her

ex-boyfriends when she'd seen them with new girl-friends. She'd felt relieved!

'Where are you going?' Zach asked from behind her.

She turned around, feeling disorientated for a moment.

He pointed to the helicopter. 'We're going in this.'

Ashling blanched.

'You've never been in a helicopter before?'

She shook her head, both terrified and exhilarated at the thought, all thoughts of Zach in bed with another woman forgotten for a second.

'Come on.' He held out a hand.

Ashling looked at it suspiciously. Then she told herself she was being ridiculous. She put her hand in his and let him lead her over to the small sleek craft. He stowed her bag and helped her up, showing her how to buckle herself in, helping fasten the belt across her chest when she was all fingers and thumbs.

He was so close she could smell him. Remember how he'd tasted. An awful yearning aching settled inside her.

Before he moved away and before she could stop herself Ashling blurted out, 'Were you with someone in Madrid?'

He stopped. Looked at her. She was glad she couldn't see his eyes. Or he hers. After a long moment that had Ashling's nerves screaming, he shook his head.

'No—not unless you count a bunch of fellow financiers.'

The relief was so immense she almost felt dizzy. Which was crazy because she had no jurisdiction over this man. And was it her imagination or was there the tiniest smile playing around the corner of his mouth as he walked away? *Damn.* If she hadn't exposed herself before now, she just done it spectacularly.

'You're the pilot?' Ashling squeaked a few minutes later, when Zach got into the front right-hand seat.

The other man got in on the left-hand side and Zach looked back at Ashling. There was a definite small smile playing around his mouth now, not helping to settle her nerves much at all.

'I only have a few hours left to log to get my pilot's licence. This is Steve, my instructor. He'll bring the helicopter back.'

Ashling smiled weakly at the other man. Then she was being instructed to put on her headphones, and they were lifting into the air with a little wobble.

Zach was obviously a bit of an adrenalin junkie—the Aston Martin, the motorbike, now the helicopter. Ashling didn't like the way this intrigued her more than it should. She couldn't just roll her eyes and pass it off as a rich man's playthings, because she had a very real sense that he didn't take any of this for granted—and that didn't fit with the man she'd believed him to be.

Ashling had been blown away by the view of London from the air, with the Thames snaking between iconic landmarks that had looked like toys far down below. But now they were in lush green countryside and she noticed that they were circling over an area with a grand house in the centre of some woodland and a garden. It was possibly one of the most idyllic scenes Ashling had ever seen.

As the helicopter descended she could see that the house was a classic redbrick Georgian manor, sur-

rounded by bucolic countryside as far as the eye could
see. There was a lake near the house, beyond the trees,
and a walled garden and an orchard. A marquee was
obviously being set up for the function. People were
milling about.

And then she spotted an outdoor swimming pool
with a pool house, tucked away in another corner of
the garden.

To Ashling's shock and surprise, a well of emotion
caught her off-guard. She'd dreamed of a forever-house
like this ever since she was a little girl, living in the
basement of Cassie's father's grand house in Belgravia.

They landed in an empty field just a little way off
from the house, where a staff member met them with
a golf buggy.

Ashling was very aware of Zach's hard body next to
hers as the small vehicle went over the bumpy ground,
knocking them off-balance and into each other.

When they approached the back of the majestic
house the full impact of the grounds and the level of
work going into the function that would take place the
following night was apparent.

They got out of the golf buggy and walked along a
winding path towards the house through the garden.

Finishing touches were being put to an area that
looked as if it would be a dance floor. Ashling caught
a glimpse inside the marquee, where it looked as if an
army of interior decorators were hanging up swathes
of material and putting out tables and chairs.

There was a huge expanse of garden blooming with
flowers of every colour from the rainbow. The scents,
even from a distance, were heady. This was exactly the
kind of garden she adored. A little bit wild. Unstruc-

tured. And a terrace ran the length of the back of the house, where gardeners were artfully twining foliage and flowers along a wall to create a backdrop.

'Wow,' Ashling said. 'I didn't realise this would be so elaborate.'

An attractive slim woman with short silver-grey hair, who looked to be in her sixties, approached them from a back door. Zach embraced her easily and smiled.

'Diana, everything seems to be in order.'

The woman smiled back. 'Exactly as a Zachary Temple event should be.'

Zach turned to Ashling. who'd come to a stop beside him. 'Ashling, this is Diana, my housekeeper. She and her husband Rob take care of pretty much everything here for me.'

As Ashling smiled and shook the woman's hand Zach was saying, 'Ashling is a friend of Cassie's who has kindly stepped in temporarily while Cassie is abroad and her PA is out of the office.'

'Nice to meet you, Ashling.'

Ashling liked the woman on sight. 'You too, Diana.'

Zach said, 'Diana will show you to your room. I'll take a quick look around while you're settling in. This afternoon I have a meeting with Georgios, and this evening we'll have dinner with him and Elena.'

'They've arrived and had lunch,' Diana told Zach. 'They're resting in their suite now.'

Diana led Ashling into the house. She wasn't sure what she'd expected, but the manor's interiors were open and airy, with polished parquet floors and elegant soft furnishings. Tasteful antiques dotted the downstairs reception rooms and bold modern art popped from the walls, providing a contrast.

The décor reminded her of the apartment in Paris. *Where she could have slept with Zach if she hadn't had a fit of sanity.* She couldn't seem to recall why it had been a bad idea. But the moment was gone now. All she'd done was remind Zach that he didn't really want her.

Diana took Ashling up to the first floor and stopped outside a door, opening it. 'These are your rooms, my dear.'

Ashling walked into the plushest, most luxurious bedroom she'd ever seen. A massive four poster bed dominated the room, dressed in soft blues and greys. Her feet almost disappeared into the carpet, it was so thick. There was an ottoman at the end of the bed, and through a doorway was an en suite bathroom that took her breath away. A romantic rolltop bath, and a marble floor matched with marble sinks and discreet silver fittings. Modern elegance in a house that had to be two hundred years old at least.

And there was a dressing room.

After the Paris apartment, Ashling wasn't all that surprised to see a selection of clothes hanging up. Dresses, men's shirts and suits. Also casual wear. She saw brand-new jeans and women's shirts and cashmere sweaters. Even raincoats.

Diana said, 'Zach employs a local boutique to keep a stock of clothes at the house, in case a guest stays over, or there is a mishap at one of his parties and someone needs to change. We keep them in this dressing room—I hope that's not an issue?'

Cassie shook her head. 'No, of course not.'

'Feel free to help yourself if you need something to wear this evening.'

Ashling saw long shimmering gowns in bright hues and her fingers itched to explore, but she said almost reluctantly, 'I've got everything I need with me, but thank you.'

Unable to resist, when Diana had left Ashling explored a little more. She guessed this floor was where the guest bedrooms were. There was a set of stairs at the end of the corridor and she went up them, finding that they led into another corridor.

From a window up there she could see the outdoor pool, its water shimmering under the afternoon sun. The blue mosaic tiles glistening under the water made it look very enticing. Diana had told her that she should feel free to use it and to help herself to swimwear from the dressing room at the pool house.

The sheer luxury of this place was truly intimidating—and this was after she'd seen Zach's London townhouse and his Paris apartment.

She heard a sound from behind a doorway—the low rumble of a voice. She walked closer. The voice stopped. She moved and a board under her foot creaked. The door opened. Zach.

'Sorry, I was being nosy.'

He stood back. 'Come in.'

Ashling went in, curious, and saw that it must be Zach's office. Actually, it was a suite of rooms. It was a masculine space. Dark furniture. Floor-to-ceiling shelves. She could see through to what looked like a boardroom with a big table, and there was another room with a couch and armchairs. A TV with the news on mute.

'You could run an industry from here,' Ashling noted.

'I do.'

Zach was leaning back against his desk, arms folded. Watching her. She felt self-conscious. 'Sorry, you're busy. Is there anything I can do? Check on the event plans?'

'I have an event manager, and Diana is pretty much in control of everything else.'

'Okay…do you need me to do anything for your meeting with Mr Stephanides?'

Zach shook his head. 'No, it's very informal—just he and I, here in my office.'

Ashling felt as if Zach knew something she didn't. It made her nervous. 'I don't think you really need me here at all. Maybe I should go.'

'You're here because Mr Stephanides requested that you be here.'

And because he didn't trust her.

The thought that those were the only reasons she was here made her feel prickly now more than nervous. 'But I don't even work for you—not really. I think you just enjoy watching me dance to your tune. Anyone could have done what I've done these past few days.'

'We haven't lied to Georgios. He knows you're only a temporary employee… But you have a point. I don't think we need to fool ourselves any longer.'

'Fool ourselves about what? The fact that I'm not really an employee at all and the only reason I'm here is because you want to punish me and you don't trust me?'

He inclined his head slightly. 'All of that—and the fact that we're ignoring the elephant in the room. The only way your debt will be fully paid to both our satisfaction.'

The last time Zach had said something like this she'd misinterpreted him, but this time she didn't think she had it wrong. And this time she wasn't indignant… she was something much more ambiguous.

'What exactly are you saying, Zach? Why am I here?'

'Because I need you for this deal and because I want you.'

Heat bloomed in her belly. Between her legs. Under her skin. 'I thought we discussed this. You agreed it wasn't a good idea… Cassie—'

'Cassie has nothing to do with this. We're two adults who have insane chemistry. We don't have to answer to anyone.'

Ashling lifted her chin. 'You think I still owe you a debt.'

Zach pushed off the desk and started to walk around her. She held herself very still, even though every cell seemed to have developed a magnetic urge to go towards him.

'What I think is that there's a certain karmic beauty to the fact that you will help me achieve a deal now when you helped me lose one four years ago. And, even though it's four years too late, you'll take the place of the lover you also helped me lose.'

'I'm sure you've had many replacements since then.' Ashling was surprised at the caustic tone in her voice.

He stood in front of her. 'Of course…but none I've wanted as much as I want you.'

Ashling desperately wished those words didn't have any effect on her. But they did.

She wanted to dent that insufferable arrogance. 'What if I don't want you?'

'You really want to go there? Make me show you up as a liar?' He glanced at his watch. 'Georgios is on his way up here right now. We can either give him a show or you can stop playing games. We both feel it, Ashling, as inconvenient as it is and as much as we might not even like each other.'

He took a step closer. Ashling could smell him. Musky and masculine. Could see stubble on his jaw. That hard mouth with its sensual lower lip. Her heart beat fast. If he kissed her now he would prove her resistance to be the sham it was.

She heard voices outside.

Zach arched a brow. 'What's it to be?'

The voices were closer now. Ashling recognised Diana's voice and a much lower, accented one. Georgios Stephanides. Feeling a sense of panic and desperation mixed with excitement, she said, 'Okay, fine. I admit it. I want you too. But I can't just... How would this work...? For how long...?'

Zach put a hand around her neck, under her hair, and tugged her close. He pressed a swift hot kiss to her mouth and pulled back. 'Don't overthink it, hmm? This lasts as long as it takes to burn out. I predict it'll be short and hot.'

He took his hand away as his words sank in and her mouth burned. And at that moment Diana showed Mr Stephanides into the room.

He saw Ashling. 'My dear! How lovely to see you again. I'm so glad you're here. I warn you that my wife is going to beg for a private yoga lesson.'

Ashling greeted the older man, genuinely pleased

to see him in spite of the undercurrents flowing between her and Zach. And that incendiary kiss. What she'd just agreed to.

'Of course your wife can have a yoga lesson. I'll go and chat with her now.' She was eager to put some space between her and Zach so she could fully absorb what had just happened.

Mr Stephanides looked at Zach. 'I'm not taking her away from doing anything important for you, am I?

Zach smiled at Ashling and it was wicked. 'Oh, no, Ashling is fully briefed. She knows exactly what I need her to do.'

CHAPTER EIGHT

THAT EVENING, ASHLING was still rattled—even though she'd done a yoga practice with Elena Stephanides. She hadn't seen Zach again. He'd been in his office with Georgios for the rest of the day.

She looked at herself in the mirror. She looked flushed. Bright-eyed. *Was she really going to do this? Embark on an affair with Zachary Temple?* What had he said? That it would be short and hot...

Maybe that was what she needed after two earnest but admittedly dull relationships that had been based on all the things she'd thought were important. Like mutual respect. Compatibility. Things in common.

Maybe those things didn't matter for a short and hot affair.

After all, as Zach had said, they didn't even have to like each other. There was something very freeing about that. Even if Ashling had to admit uncomfortably that her feelings for Zach were a lot more ambiguous than they had been before.

She looked at herself in the mirror. The cocktail dress was cream silk and chiffon with a ruched and sweetheart-edged bodice, it fell in chiffon folds to just below her knees. The halter neck straps were encrusted with pearls and crossed over her bare back. The only jewellery she wore was a necklace her mother had given her. An Algerian love knot.

She slipped on a pair of black high heels and before she could lose her nerve—or, as Zach had warned her, *overthink it*—Ashling took a deep breath and left the room.

Zach couldn't remember the last time he'd felt such a sense of anticipation. It was even eclipsing the fact that Georgios Stephanides had finally agreed to do the deal. Their legal teams were going to travel down from London first thing tomorrow and contracts would be signed.

The old man had looked at him earlier, after their last intense round of negotiations, and he'd said to Zach, 'I'm glad I've seen you here, in this place. To be perfectly frank, I've been reluctant to sign a deal till now because I didn't really think you could understand the importance of the legacy I'm handing you… To put it bluntly, you're a lone wolf, Zach. And lone wolves are dangerous. They're unpredictable. But you were smart to invite me here,' he'd continued. 'This house…is a home. Or it will be one day. I feel that very much. And Ashling—'

Zach had cut in, in shock at Georgios's blunt insight. 'Ashling is just—'

The man had put a hand up. 'I might be old, Zach, but I'm not blind yet. I can see the passion between you.'

A familiar but for the first time unsavoury ruthlessness had urged Zach to stay quiet in that moment. After all, the man was right. There was something between him and Ashling. He just didn't know how finite it would be.

And as for this place being a *home* some day... That concept made Zach feel a little winded. And yet he couldn't deny the irrational desire he'd had when he'd seen this house. To buy it even though it stuck out of his property portfolio like a sore thumb.

Georgios had continued. 'I've seen here that the lone wolf can be tamed, and *that* is why I will do the deal with you.'

Ridiculous, Zach thought to himself now, as he waited for his guests to arrive for dinner. *Georgios Stephanides is a romantic old fool. That's all.*

He poured himself an aperitif and just then heard a sound from behind him. Even before he turned he knew it was her.

She was standing in the doorway. Hesitant. Before, he'd suspected it was artifice, but he recognised it now. Because for a long time he'd had to consciously battle his own feelings of inadequacy. Of feeling that he didn't belong in places like this. She had it too.

She looked like a vision in cream and silk, her skin lightly golden. Absurdly, an urge to protect rose up in him. To reassure. Zach shoved it down. There was no place for that here.

'Would you like a drink?' he asked.

She stepped over the threshold, her legs slim and shapely. Bare. Lust surged, hot and uncontrollable, at the thought of those legs wrapped around him, her body milking—

'White wine would be nice, thank you.'

Even her voice, soft and husky, caught at him. It was

as if now that he'd decided to give free rein to his desire it was morphing out of his control. Almost.

He poured her a drink and told himself to get it together. He was more sophisticated than this.

When he'd handed her the drink he said, 'You look beautiful.'

Her cheeks pinkened. 'Thank you.'

She seemed skittish. Avoiding his eye. Zach was used to women being forward, confident. Especially if they knew he wanted them. But Ashling wasn't emboldened by the knowledge that Zach had exhibited his weakness for her. In his world, any kind of vulnerability was ruthlessly exploited. He wanted her to look at him, wanted to see her eyes.

'Ash—'

'Good evening. I hope we haven't kept you waiting?'

Zach cursed silently as the Stephanides made their appearance.

Ashling sent up silent thanks when the other couple arrived. She'd watched Zach for an unguarded moment before he'd turned around to see her. Hovering on the threshold…beset for a moment by old insecurities. It had been a reminder that she didn't belong in a world like this. That she didn't fit…

Unwelcome memories had come…one in particular.

She'd been waiting for Cassie to come home from school one day, and when she'd heard the car arrive back at house in Belgravia she'd run upstairs, excited to see her friend. She'd burst into the hall as Cassie had arrived—only to be hauled backwards by the rough hand of Cassie's father, whom she hadn't seen emerging from the library.

He'd loomed over her, a powerful, intimidating man. 'Who said you could come into this part of the house?'

Cassie had cut in plaintively, 'But, Dad—'

He'd looked at his daughter, 'Upstairs, Cassandra. Now. I've told you that if you want to see Ashling you can play in the garden or in her quarters.'

The embarrassment was still vivid. She'd laughed about it afterwards with Cassie, but she'd never forgotten the awful feeling of shame. Of feeling that she didn't belong.

Elena Stephanides gasped, bringing Ashling back from the lingering wisps of the past. 'My dear girl, is that a Chanel dress?'

Ashling smiled. 'Yes, it is. It's vintage. I found it in a charity shop in Mayfair.'

The other woman sighed theatrically. 'I don't even want to know how much you paid for it, because I can still remember the original price when it was brand-new!'

Ashling laughed, grateful for this buffer between her and the brooding intensity coming from Zach. She knew it was too late to resist what was inevitable. *She didn't want to resist.* But that didn't stop her from being very afraid that he would consume her utterly and reveal just how flimsy her defences really were.

Because the truth was she'd never risked her heart before—even if she'd fooled herself into thinking she had.

And to risk her heart was to risk being humiliated, like her mother had been. Humiliated and rejected. Cast aside because she didn't belong. She'd prided herself on being more savvy. But she hadn't been tested. Until now.

* * *

'Come here.'

A delicious shiver skated over Ashling's skin at Zach's request. Dinner was over. Their digestif drinks in the sitting room were finished. The Stephanides had just retired.

Over the course of the evening Ashling's concerns had faded more and more into the background, replaced by growing heat and tension. She'd never been so conscious of another human being before. She was aware of every tiny gesture Zach made. The way he sat back in his chair and lazily held his wine glass. The way he smiled. The way his eyes slid to her when the other couple were talking to one another.

She'd felt herself blooming more and more under each successive glance and look. Like a flower opening up to the sun. It was heady.

Seeing him interact with Georgios and Elena, relaxed and charming, showed Ashling just how devastatingly irresistible he could be. She didn't have a hope. And he hadn't even had to seduce her. He'd had her from the moment she'd stood in front of him four years ago and set in train this chain of events.

She sat in a chair at right angles to the couch where the older couple had sat. Zach was in a chair at the other end. She felt a need to resist, even though she knew it was futile. Zach was just too…assured.

As if sensing her resistance, he sat forward, relaxed and yet primed. She could sense his tension. It mirrored hers.

'Come here, Ashling.'

She'd never been so conscious of her name and how it sounded.

'Why should I come to you?'

Zach arched a brow. He stood up, uncoiling his tall body. He closed the distance and stood in front of her. And then, to her surprise, he went down on his knees before her.

'Better?' he asked.

Suddenly she couldn't breathe. Zach put his hands on her knees, watching her.

He pushed her knees apart slightly. 'Okay?'

Something about his solicitude relaxed the knot inside her. She nodded.

He pushed her knees apart more and moved forward, coming between her thighs. He ran his hands up her bare thighs under her dress. Every nerve-ending screamed with tension.

He said, 'I want to see you.'

Ashling lifted trembling hands and undid the tiny hooks that held the pearl-encrusted straps to the bodice of the dress at the front. The bodice sagged, and after another explicit look from Zach Ashling nodded.

Zach took his hands off her thighs and lifted them to the dress. He slowly pulled down the bodice, exposing her to his dark gaze. She'd never been more conscious of her modest-sized breasts. They felt heavy, the nipples tightening to sharp points of need.

He spread his hands around her back, urging her forward slightly so that she sat down in the cradle of the chair. And then he bent forward, placing his mouth first on one breast and then the other. His tongue laved the peaks, his teeth tugging gently on skin so sensitised that Ashling bit her lip to stop crying out.

Her hands were in Zach's hair, holding tight. She

was torn between pushing him away when it got too much and never letting him go.

He left her breasts and Ashling's blurry eyes focused. His face was flushed. Eyes glittering. He moved back, but not far, and pushed the skirt of her dress up. He pushed her thighs apart even more and sat back on his haunches, looking at her.

The only thing stopping her from trying to close her legs was the naked hunger in Zach's gaze. She'd never seen anything like it.

He reached forward and pulled her underwear to one side. Every drop of heat in Ashling's body migrated to that spot.

She could only watch as Zach's dark head moved down and she felt his breath feather along her inner thigh, his mouth pressing open-mouthed kisses to skin she'd never thought of as sensitive before.

She was squirming as he came closer and closer to the centre of her body. He put a hand on her belly, holding her still, as he all but lifted her with his other hand and placed his mouth right between her legs.

Ashling was barely aware of his hand moving up to cup her breast, kneading her flesh, trapping a nipple between his fingers, as his mouth and tongue explored her secret folds of flesh with a thoroughness that left her shaking.

She put a fist to her mouth to try and stop the sounds leaking out…hoarse screams. Tension spiralled deep inside her and she tried desperately to cling on, not to let herself shatter, because it seemed very important to avoid shattering at all costs.

But it was impossible. With one flick of Zach's

tongue Ashling's world exploded into a million pieces and she was undone.

She was vaguely aware of Zach pulling her dress back up over her breasts. She looked at him as he stood up. She felt dizzy. Waves of pleasure throbbed under her skin.

He reached for her hands, tugging her up and out of the chair. Much to her mortification, her legs wobbled. He immediately scooped her up into his arms as if she weighed nothing.

He took her into the dimly lit hallway. All was quiet. Preparations for the event had stopped hours before. Ashling felt deliciously lethargic. She knew she should probably object to being carried in Zach's arms, but his chest was so solid and her arms fitted around his neck as if they'd always been there.

He climbed the stairs with ease, bringing Ashling down to the end of the hall, past her bedroom and others.

He opened a door and Ashling had the impression of a corner suite…windows overlooking the property on two sides…a massive bed dressed in dark colours.

Zach put her down. Her shoes were…somewhere. She vaguely remembered kicking them off after dinner, having a conversation with Elena about the discomfort of high heels.

Her dress was still loose around her chest and Zach moved behind her, carefully lowering the zip. The dress fell down under its own weight, around her feet.

Now she wore nothing but her underwear.

Zach came back in front of her and his eyes were heavy-lidded. He trailed a finger across one shoulder and down her arm. Traced the side of one breast. 'You are beautiful.'

Ashling ducked her head, her hair falling forward. He put a finger under her chin and urged her to look up. He seemed to want to say something, but then he just cupped her face in his hands, and his mouth was covering hers, and a new hunger licked at her blood, seeking more. Much more.

She felt Zach shed his clothes, cursing against her mouth when a button wouldn't open. She heard it *pop* and land somewhere. She felt like giggling.

But she didn't feel like giggling when Zach stood in front of her naked.

He was majestic. All the way from the corded muscles of his shoulders, down to his chest and his slim hips, where his erection was long and thick and hard.

Ashling's mouth dried.

His thighs were powerful. Long legs planted like a warrior. He was completely unashamed. And why shouldn't he be? He was exquisite.

Overcome with a feeling of awe and curiosity, Ashling whispered, 'Can I touch you?'

His jaw clenched. He nodded.

Ashling tentatively put out a hand to his chest, exploring the warm skin over steely muscles, the curve of his pectoral muscles and the ridges that ran below. The dark line of hair that dissected his lower belly.

She moved around to his back, broad and strong. His taut buttocks. And then returned to his front. She looked at him. At the evidence of how much he wanted her. Instinctively, she reached out and wrapped her hand around him lightly. Veins ran under the delicate skin. Moisture beaded at the head.

'Ash...if you keep touching me like that this will be over very quickly. And I have no intention of letting that happen.' Zach sounded tortured.

Ash.

Her heart beat faster. She took her hand away and Zach led her over to the bed.

She lay down and watched him looking at her. She felt a heady rush of feminine power. And then he came down on his hands over her and showed her all too easily who really held the power here.

He explored her body like a man discovering new territory. Every dip and hollow was traced. He paid homage to her breasts for long, luxurious minutes. He dispensed with her underwear, delved back between her legs, exploring with his fingers this time.

Her back was arching off the bed. His mouth was on hers, his fingers pushing her to the edge of her control, but it wasn't enough.

She pulled back. Zach looked at her. 'Please,' she said, 'I want *you*.'

His eyes glittered. For a second she thought she saw something like a flash of triumph, but she couldn't decipher the enigmatic look. She was too needy right now. She'd never known it could be like this. All-consuming. Desperate.

Zach reached for something and she heard foil rip. He smoothed protection onto his erection and moved over her, nudging her legs apart.

Ashling sucked in a breath when Zach breached her body.

He stopped. 'We'll take this slow, okay?'

She nodded, once again disconcerted by his consideration. She didn't know what she'd expected, but in her limited experience of lovemaking she had felt as if it was a man's journey, not necessarily a mutual one, or even hers. But this was a world apart.

Zach joined their bodies with a slow, deliberate movement, giving her time to adjust. He was big. He took her breath away. For a moment the sensation almost bordered on painful, but as if sensing that Zach pulled out and then eased back in again. And this time Ashling breathed out.

It was amazing.

An instinct as old as time took over as Ashling's body adjusted to Zach's and she moved beneath him, wordlessly telling him he could go faster, be less gentle.

A big hand caught her thigh, lifting it up. He went deeper and Ashling made a helpless sound of pleasure. Perspiration covered her skin as her entire being became consumed with this moment, this man, and the storm of sensation gathering inside her, coiling tighter and tighter as Zach's movements became less considered and more elemental.

She was climbing and climbing, begging incoherently, pleading...

Zach pulled out and she looked up at him, half-crazed. 'Please, Zach...'

He surged back into her body and Ashling tipped over into a place of such extreme pleasure she blacked out for a second.

When she became aware of her surroundings again, Ashling felt Zach pulling something over her—a soft, light cover. She was so stunned by what had just happened, and by the waves of pleasure that still pulsed inside her, that she couldn't help confiding, 'I didn't know it could be like that...'

* * *

Zach went still. He was leaning on his elbow beside Ashling. Her eyes were closed. Her words had been almost slurred, as if she was drunk. But he'd heard her. Her body was covered now, but he knew that after what had just happened every line of her physique would be burnt onto his brain.

The truth was, he hadn't known that it could be like that either. His body was still humming with an overload of pleasure. He was still—after what had felt like the most intense orgasm of his life—semi-aroused.

He waited for a sense satisfaction to hit, recalling how she'd been completely at his mercy, begging for release. And she had begged. Her eyes had been wide and desperate, breath coming fast. She had been totally at his mercy. But any sense of satisfaction was elusive.

And at the time of her capitulation, Zach had barely noticed.

Because the edges of his own control had been badly fraying. The moment had come and gone before he'd even really realised its significance, drowned out in the desperate pursuit of a pleasure so mind-altering that he could only put it down to an anomalous freak of chemistry.

Short and hot. That was what he'd told Ashling.

It had definitely been hot. The only problem was that right now Zach couldn't foresee just how short it might be. He had an uncomfortable feeling that he'd just unleashed a hunger that wouldn't be easily sated.

When Ashling woke there were pink tendrils kissing the sky outside. Dawn. She was disorientated. Her body felt…different. *Good*. Heavy… Hungry, yet sated. A strange contrast.

And then there was a movement in the bed beside her and it all came flooding back in glorious Technicolor. She held her breath and turned her head. Zach was on his back asleep, an arm thrown over his head. His chest was bare, and a sheet rode strategically low on his hips, showing the start of dark curling hair where the sheet tented over an impressive bulge, even at rest.

Heat curled into Ashling's belly and between her legs, where she felt tender.

She looked at his face. He looked younger in sleep. Lashes long and dark. Those dark, watchful eyes hidden. She imagined him waking and finding her looking at him. That galvanised her to steal from the bed as quietly as she could.

She pulled on her dress, just to cover up, and picked up her underwear. Back in her own room, she slumped against the closed door. The full magnitude of what had happened sank in. How amazing it had been. How considerate Zach had been. How she did have a capacity for pleasure—extreme pleasure.

She thought of Zach's prediction that this would be *short and hot*. She almost hoped that Zach was right. Last night had been so intense, and totally unexpected. Surely, she thought a little desperately, that had been a one-off. Not every time would be like that? It had been a culmination of everything between them since they'd met again…that was all.

The thought of sleeping with Zach again, now that she knew what to expect, alternately excited and terrified her. She'd been so exposed. So needy. So ravenous. It was a side to her that she hadn't known existed and it scared her slightly, because it hinted at a level of passion in which she could lose herself. Forget to protect herself. Forget the lessons she'd learnt about not falling for the wrong person.

In all honesty, she didn't know if she could withstand a prolonged period of Zach's seduction. She had a very real fear that she would be incinerated in the process.

Zach couldn't quite believe his eyes. At the end of the garden, tucked away from prying eyes, well away from the hubbub of people preparing for the party that night, Ashling was giving a yoga class to Elena Stephanides. They both had yoga mats and Ashling was standing on one leg now, with the other one bent, her foot tucked against her inner thigh, arms outstretched.

Elena was mirroring her pose. But all Zach could see was Ashling. Every lithe and toned inch of her petite body. He'd felt her strength last night. The power in her thighs, clamped around his waist as the inner muscles of her body had contracted around his so forcibly that he'd—

'Zach?'

It was as if someone had dumped a bucket of cold water over his head. What on earth was he doing?

He turned around. Georgios Stephanides was looking at him with a far too knowing twinkle in his eye. He was holding out a heavy silver ink pen.

'Time to sign—unless, that is, you've changed your mind?'

No way, thought Zach, pushing all thoughts of a lithe temptress out of his mind.

He sat down and took the pen, and scrawled his

name beside Georgios's. He waited for the surge of satisfaction to come. After all, this deal blew everything else out of the water, and after this there would be no doubt that Zach had taken his place among his ancestors, whether his family liked to admit it or not. They wouldn't be able to deny it—or deny him his rightful place.

Satisfaction was there. But it was hollow. Almost an anti-climax. Which made him think of another climax. One a few hours before, that had almost seared his brain clear of everything he'd ever known.

Georgios clapped him on the shoulder. Zach looked up.

'Take care of my legacy, Zach,' the man said. 'Don't make me regret what I've done here today.'

Before, Zach would have spoken some platitude. He'd done it a million times before in similar situations. But for the first time he felt an echoing of the older man's emotion inside him. Georgios Stephanides didn't really know Zach. They shared no blood. And yet he'd shown a level of trust in Zach that his own flesh and blood never had.

He stood up, shook Georgios's hand, feeling surprisingly humbled. 'Thank you. I will.'

Georgios and the rest of their teams left the boardroom attached to his study. Zach took a breath. He was losing it. Going soft. Great sex had never had this effect on him before. He'd also never woken in his bed after a woman had left it. Usually he was the one to put very clear boundaries in place. He was the one to leave.

A sense of foreboding prickled over his skin.

He went back to the window and looked out. Ashling was bent like a triangle now, with her Lycra-clad bottom in the air. And just like that, any sense of fore-boding melted into a haze of heat.

The first piece of karma had just been served. The second piece was *her*. In his bed again. For as long as this heat continued. And then he would be free to move on, unencumbered by any ghosts from the past.

Maybe Georgios Stephanides was right, and this house would be a home one day. But it would not be a home for the type of family that had shunned Zach since he was born. It would be for a family that would cement Zach's legacy in society, and make all the sacrifices that had led to this moment, worth it.

CHAPTER NINE

IT WAS HER dream dress. A fairy-tale concoction of cream silk, lace and tulle, covered with huge embroidered gorgeous colourful flowers in reds and pinks and dark mulberry. Loose sleeves came down to her elbows, with lace trims. A layer of dark pink tulle also covered in appliquéd flowers fell to the ground.

It was breathtaking.

And Ashling couldn't resist it.

She'd never seen anything so whimsical and romantic in her life. She felt like a princess.

The dress was one that had been sent over from the boutique. It had caught her eye a few times, so she'd pulled it out, and before she'd been able to stop herself she'd been trying it on. Just to see…

And now it was on and it was as if it had been made especially for her. The temptation to wear it was huge, and yet she felt guilty. Even though Diana had told her to help herself to anything.

The dress she'd been planning on wearing was the black silk one she'd worn the previous weekend. Normally Ashling would take pride in reusing clothes, not sniffy about being judged. But now it looked drab and cheap.

A voice whispered to her. *You want to wear this because you feel romantic after last night. Because you want romance...with Zach Temple.*

Immediately Ashling went to open the catch at the back of the dress, to take it off, but then something rebellious flamed to life in her belly. Was it so bad to feel romantic? To want romance?

She found Zach more and more intriguing. They'd slept together. And that had been...earth-shattering. Yet she wasn't deluding herself for a second that there was anything beyond the purely physical happening here. So was it so bad to want to indulge in this moment? To feel beautiful? Desired?

Ashling made a face at herself. She was being ridiculous. It was just a dress. And after looking out of the window and seeing the guests start to arrive she needed all the glamorous armour she could get.

She hadn't seen Zach all day. He'd been in his office suite with Georgios Stephanides and their legal teams. She looked out of the window one more time to see if she could see him.

The garden had been transformed into a wonderland. It was a gorgeous summer's evening. The sky was vast and turning to dusk. Fairy lights in trees and flaming lanterns illuminated the darkening space. Small tables and chairs were dotted around. She could see the dance floor. A canopy of lights was strung from the trees to cover the space. It was like the setting for a Shakespeare play, or a film set.

Then she saw him, and her heart hitched before she could stop it. He was wearing a white dinner jacket and black bow-tie. He stood out, and once again Ashling felt a little pang at seeing him look somehow…isolated, even though he was surrounded by people.

As if sensing her regard, he turned his head and looked up, directly at her window. Ashling shrank back, heart thumping. But she couldn't hide up here for ever.

She found a pair of pink silk high-heeled sandals, and at the last minute picked up a yellow silk flower and pinned it in her hair on one side, where she'd gathered it up into a rough low bun. And then, steeling herself to see Zach for the first time since she'd left his bed that morning, she made her way to the party.

Where the hell was she?

The need to see Ashling gnawed at Zach like a physical craving. People were arriving. Surrounding him with their fake smiles and the sycophancy which he'd become inured to over the years…

And then, just when he was about to go in search of her, he saw her on the terrace, near the French doors. She was talking to Diana. Her hair was pulled back, showing off her delicate bone structure. And her dress…

Her dress stood out among all the monochrome, the blacks and greys and whites, in a riotous profusion of colours. He saw a flower in her hair. He found himself smiling. He shouldn't have expected anything less.

She turned and looked and found him. At the moment their eyes met Zach felt for a second as if he was losing his footing. She picked up the dress, so it wouldn't trail on the ground, and walked towards him across the lawn. The disconcerting sensation of something shifting underneath him, around him, lingered.

He shook his head. It was Georgios's mention of *home* that was messing with his head.

She reached him and her scent tickled his nostrils. Sweet and musky. It reminded him of how she'd smelt when he'd tasted her—

'You look beautiful.' He forced the words out in a bid to regain some semblance of control.

He noticed she wore no jewellery apart from the necklace she'd worn the previous night. A kind of love knot. Clearly of sentimental value. That snagged in his brain, but he pushed it aside for now.

'Thank you.' She looked shy. Then she gestured to the dress. 'It's one of yours.'

Zach arched a brow. 'Really? I didn't know tulle was my thing.'

She realised what she'd said, and laughed. Zach was aware of people turning to look. He wanted to snatch her away.

'No, sorry—not like that. I mean, it's one of the dresses you have sent from the boutique. For guests.'

For his lover.

The dress could have been made for her. Impulsively, because he wasn't usually inclined to give gifts to lovers in case they got the wrong idea, he said, 'Keep it. It suits you.'

Her eyes widened, and then some expression that Zach couldn't decipher crossed her face. She shuttered it quickly.

'No…but thank you. I'll arrange to have it cleaned… after…'

Zach shied away from trying to figure out what that expression had meant. He privately thought it would be a miracle if the dress survived intact. He couldn't see any obvious fastenings, and anticipation was already firing his blood. He remembered waking and finding her gone that morning and that prickle of exposure.

'You were gone this morning.'

She looked contrite. 'I woke and… The truth is that I didn't know if you'd appreciate waking and finding me still there. I wasn't sure what you'd expect. I thought you'd want your space.'

It was the first time a lover had wanted to give him space. The irony that he hadn't appreciated it wasn't lost on him.

He said, 'What I wanted was *you.*'

'Still?'

He almost didn't hear it, her voice was so low. He looked at her, wondering if she was fishing for reassurance. But she looked genuinely uncertain.

'Yes, still.' The fact that it wasn't patently obvious how much he hungered for her was comforting.

A waiter stopped beside them and Zach took two glasses of champagne, handing her one. If she was reacting to him telling her explicitly that he still wanted her, it wasn't evident on her face.

He said, 'I'm celebrating.'

She looked at him, comprehension dawning. 'The deal? With Georgios Stephanides?'

He nodded, feeling a mixture of exposure and pride. Usually these victories were solo affairs. For the first time he felt the need to share it.

She took his hand, moved closer. 'Zach, that's amazing. Congratulations.'

He gave in to an urge too powerful to ignore. He bent down and covered her mouth with his. She was tense.

He pulled back. He saw the desire in her eyes, but she said, 'I thought you wouldn't want people to see… to know…'

He shook his head. 'Come here.'

Something flared in her eyes and her cheeks grew pink. He put an arm around her waist, pulling her into him. This time when he kissed her she didn't tense. She melted against him. It took all his restraint to stop the kiss. Pull back. When he did, her eyes stayed closed for a second. He uttered a silent oath.

'Zach, there you are. Mr Carmichael has just arrived. He's looking for you.'

It was Diana's voice that broke Ashling out of the lust haze in her brain. Zach still wanted her. He hadn't wanted her to leave his bed. He'd just kissed her in front of everyone.

He said, 'I'll be right there.'

Diana melted away discreetly. Ashling took a step back from Zach in a bid to try and clear her head. But he took her hand and led her with him into the crowd. She took a sip of sparkling wine, as if that might fortify her.

It only made things worse.

Zach introduced her to his guests, but he was their main focus. They simply looked at Ashling with naked curiosity.

She saw the Stephanides arrive and gestured to tell him that she would go to them, welcoming a chance to get her breath back. Zach nodded and let her go. She felt a prickle between her shoulder blades as if he was watching her leave but then she told herself she was being ridiculous.

* * *

About an hour later Zach was growing impatient again. *Where was she now?*

He'd watched her meet the Stephanides, and then a small crowd had formed around them, as if Ashling were attracting people to her by her sheer open demeanour.

He'd never been with anyone like her before. He was used to people who wouldn't dream of emoting or talking with unguarded abandon. But she literally had no agenda. Or appeared not to.

She also didn't appear to need to plaster herself to his side at all times, which was irritating. And irritating for being irritating.

He saw Georgios and Elena and extricated himself from his group of guests and went over. Elena said something about an emergency in the kitchen, and that Ashling had gone to see if she could help.

As Zach was walking to the kitchen he met Diana, who looked flustered. 'Oh, Zach, the chef has been taken to hospital with a suspected heart attack. Rob has gone with him. He'll let me know what happens, but we think he'll be okay.'

Zach said, 'Call my physician and have him on standby in case he's needed.'

'Of course.'

'Have you seen Ashling?'

Diana looked sheepish. 'She's in the kitchen.'

Zach frowned. And then he followed Diana to the kitchen—where he was greeted by the sight of organised chaos as everyone worked—with Ashling slap-bang in the middle of the confusion, wearing an apron over her dress. She was taking a tray out of the oven.

'What the hell…?'

He hadn't even realised he'd spoken out loud until Diana said, 'Ashling was with me when Rob told me what was happening and she came straight in and took over. She's amazing, Zach. Did you know she trained as a chef?'

Zach felt a mixture of shock, frustration and pride. 'She might have mentioned it at some point.'

He went over to her and she looked up, cheeks pink, distracted.

'What are you doing?'

She was unfazed. 'Keeping your guests supplied with canapés.'

He looked around at the hive of activity. 'No one else here can do that?'

'They got a fright when Marcel collapsed, and they needed someone to take over.'

'You have fifteen minutes to reassure the assistant chef that he is capable of the job and come back to the party.'

'Is that an order or a request?'

Desire twisted inside Zach at her cheeky expression. No one spoke to him like this. It was exhilarating.

He reached out and put a hand behind her neck, caressing. Suddenly she didn't look so cheeky. She was looking at his mouth.

'It's an order.'

Ashling sneaked into the back of the marquee just as Zach was delivering his speech before the charity auction. Money would be raised for local charities—chief of which was a cancer charity which, she'd discovered, he'd set up himself.

Ashling was shocked to hear him reveal now that he'd set up the cancer charity after his mother had died of a rare form of cancer. He was also involved in the local hospice, after they'd provided care for her at the end of her life.

Everyone was rapt as he spoke. And she couldn't blame them. He was mesmerising and not remotely sentimental, even though he was talking about something that was obviously deeply personal.

Ashling realised that she knew next to nothing about Zach's family. She wondered if his father was still alive. If he had siblings. He'd very skilfully deflected any focus on his personal life—which Ashling could understand, coming from her own less than conventional background.

At that moment his dark gaze pinpointed her, standing at the back of the crowd. She told herself a little desperately that Zach's family was none of her business. She didn't care about what had shaped him. She only cared about the very explicit promise in those eyes.

'Finished saving the world?'

'One canapé at a time,' Ashling quipped, her response hiding how unsettled she'd felt after hearing him talk about his mother.

After he'd delivered his speech Zach had come straight to where Ashling was standing and taken her hand, leading her out of the marquee.

She heard them start the bidding for the charity auction. 'Don't you need to be in there for that?'

He shook his head. 'It's all under control.'

She looked up at him. His face was half in shadow

in the dusky light. 'I'm sorry about your mother…you must have been close.'

'We were.'

'Your father…?'

Zach's jaw tensed. 'He's not in my life.'

Ashling guessed his parents must have divorced. Some of the guests who weren't bidding in the auction had spilled out into the garden and were taking to the dance floor, dancing to the slow, sensual rhythm of the jazz coming from the band. She spotted Georgios and Elena, looking very much in love.

Zach said, 'Thank you for helping Diana to cope with the emergency. You didn't have to do that.'

Ashling shrugged a shoulder, embarrassed. 'It was nothing.'

'Dance?'

She looked up. 'Okay.'

Zach led her over to the dance floor and swept her into his arms. Ashling caught Elena's eye and the older woman smiled indulgently. She felt like a fraud, though, next to their very obvious absorption in each other.

What she and Zach had was…*short and hot*. Not long-lasting. Enduring.

'Is that a love knot?'

Ashling looked up to see Zach was looking at her necklace. 'Yes, it's an Algerian love knot.'

'Given to you by a lover?'

Ashling was tempted to be blasé and say yes. To try and even out the inequality she felt next to this man who must have handed over hundreds of trinkets to his lovers.

But she couldn't. 'No, it was a gift from my mother. For my twenty-first birthday.'

Zach said, 'Good. I'm glad.'

Ashling couldn't stop her silly heart pounding faster at that response.

The canopy of golden lights twinkled overhead and out of the corner of her eye she could see the tulle of her dress swirling around her as Zach twirled her away from his body and then back in. She felt herself being sucked into the fantasy of believing in the romance of the moment.

But when Zach pulled her close again, and she felt her body respond helplessly to his whipcord strength, she had to remind herself that any sense of romance was fleeting and an illusion. What was happening here was purely physical.

As if to make sure she understood that, Zach pulled her even closer, and Ashling's breath stopped when she felt the press of his arousal against her belly. Desire, sharp and urgent, licked at her lower belly.

He stopped moving. She looked up at him, caught by the intensity of his gaze. The air thickened between them, tension rising. And urgency.

He caught her hand in his and was leading her off the dance floor before she could take another breath. With single-minded focus, not stopping for anyone, he led her onto the terrace and through the French doors.

It was quiet in the house, because everyone was outside in the humid summer evening.

'Zach…where are we going?'

Ashling was afraid to articulate the need building inside her. Surely it was the same for him and they had the same goal. *Now.*

He took her through one of the formal reception rooms and then through a secret door, camouflaged because it was wallpapered the same as the wall. The room he took her into was a library, with floor-to-ceiling shelves and worn leather furniture. He closed the door behind them and, still holding Ashling's hand, went and sat down on one of the big leather chairs, pulling her down onto his lap.

She landed with a flurry of silk and tulle billowing around them. Within seconds their mouths were fused, and Zach's hands were moving from Ashling's waist to her bottom. She could feel him underneath her, hard, and she moved against him.

He pulled back. 'Witch.' Then he put his hands on her waist, lifting her. 'Straddle me.'

Ashling lifted up the material of the dress and came up on her knees, either side of his thighs.

Zach put his hands on her thighs under the dress. She looked down at him. His expression was hidden in the dim light. She reached for his bow-tie, undoing it, opening his top button. She bent down, pressed a kiss to his jaw, feeling the stubble tickle her mouth. She was trying to ignore the welling of dangerous emotion.

Zach's hands left her thighs and she heard him undo his belt. There was the snap of a button, the tug of a zip.

She pulled back and came up on her knees. She could feel the heat of Zach's body. He reached between them, rubbing the silk of her underwear where it covered the centre of her.

Ashling groaned softly. The sounds of the party drifted in from outside. Laughter, music… She put her hands on his shoulders.

He tugged her underwear to one side, the movement causing delicious friction along her sensitised skin.

He asked, 'Are you tender? After last night?'

Ashling could feel herself blushing. 'A little, but it's okay.'

She heard foil rip as Zach protected himself, and then he was taking himself in his hand and nudging the head of his erection along her folds. Ashling met him, taking in a breath as she sank down. He impaled her. Slowly. Deliciously. Until she was so full she could barely breathe.

Then, with his hands on her hips, he urged her to move up and down, taking his time, setting the rhythm, letting her get used to him.

Until her own instincts took over and the need inside her grew. Her movements became faster, more urgent. Her skin grew damp, and every cell in her body strained for release. But she was afraid of the oncoming storm.

'Let go, Ash. I've got you.'

Zach reached up and tugged her head down, claiming her mouth just as the storm broke. He captured her breathy groan of release as his other hand clamped to her waist and held her still while his own body found its release inside her embrace.

The shock waves ebbed slowly. The perspiration on their skin cooled. Ashling's face was embedded on Zach's shoulder, her mouth touching his neck. She flicked out her tongue to taste his skin and, incredibly, his body jerked in response.

He huffed a laugh. Ashling smiled against his skin, a wave of satisfied exhaustion claiming her before she could stop it.

* * *

When Zach went back out to the party he felt drunk. Drunk on sex. He'd lain Ashling down on the couch in the library, covered her with a throw. It had taken all his willpower not to just carry her up to the nearest bedroom.

He'd never behaved so spontaneously. But no other woman had ever precipitated such a visceral hunger in him. A hunger that had to be assuaged immediately.

It wasn't just desire, though, a little voice reminded him uncomfortably.

No. There had been an expression in her eyes when they'd danced. Open, unguarded. Wistful. He'd acted on a powerful instinct to do whatever it took to turn that expression into something much earthier. Base.

The women he'd chosen as lovers up to now had been pragmatic. Ambitious. Well-connected. They hadn't looked at him as if they could see right into him. Or as if he was promising them something beyond a mutually satisfying liaison.

If he ever was going to settle down, then it would be with one of those women. Women who didn't stir his emotions. Women who didn't rouse old fantasies of a different life. The kind of life that had been snatched out of his grasp the moment he'd been born.

This weekend with Ashling…getting her out of his system and settling old scores…was all he needed to move forward with the next phase of his life. The deal with Georgios Stephanides was done. It was time to take his rightful place among his peers and prove to the family who'd rejected him that he was their equal.

* * *

Ashling felt disorientated when she woke the following morning. She was alone in Zach's bed.

She saw two empty champagne glasses on the bedside table and pieced together the events... After the library, she'd woken in Zach's arms last night as he'd carried her up to bed. She'd protested, saying, 'Shouldn't we get back to the party?'

He'd replied dryly, 'Most people have left...it's just a few stragglers.'

Ashling had buried her head in his chest. 'I'm sorry. I didn't mean to fall asleep like that.'

He'd brought her here, to his room. By the time she'd stood in front of him she'd been wide awake again. His bow-tie had been hanging rakishly loose. Jacket gone.

Ashling could see her dress now. The swathe of romantic silk, lace and flowers trailed over the bottom of the bed like a glorious stain of rich colours.

They'd made love again, as hungrily as if they hadn't just made love a short time before. It had scared Ashling slightly...this ravenous craving he'd awoken in her.

They'd woken during the night, ravenous again except this time for food. They'd gone down to the kitchen and eaten leftovers from the party. Zach had given Ashling a pair of his sweatpants and a T-shirt. She'd rolled the pants up and tied the T-shirt into a knot at her midriff.

They'd come back to the bedroom as dawn was breaking, with two glasses of champagne. And then made love again.

Ashling's body felt deliciously heavy. Sated. Tender. She was just wondering where Zach might be when she heard a noise and looked up, to see him walking out of the bathroom with nothing but a towel hitched around his waist.

Her mouth dried. His skin was gleaming, muscles bunching as he rubbed his hair with a smaller towel. Ashling's belly tightened. Again.

He saw her. Took the towel from his head. He was clean-shaven again. 'Morning…'

'Hi.' Ashling felt ridiculously shy, considering the fact that this man knew her more intimately than anyone else in the world. Even her previous boyfriends. Safe to say that Zach's very thorough brand of lovemaking meant that he'd touched, caressed, kissed, licked, nipped every part of her body.

He stood at the end of the bed. 'I've decided to stay for the weekend.'

Ashling's insides contracted. *It was over.* Already. She shouldn't be surprised, really. Even though every successive time they'd made love it had just got better and better.

For her.

She had to remember that she was a novice compared to Zach. He was probably bored already.

She saw the discarded T-shirt nearby and reached for it, pulling it on back to front. She didn't care. She felt a bit panicky now.

'Okay, that's cool. I can get a train from the nearest village—or maybe one of the event people will be going back into town. I can get a lift with—'

He frowned. 'What are you talking about?'

'You said you're staying for the weekend. I presumed…' She trailed off, and watched as he dropped the smaller towel and stalked around the side of the bed.

'What I should have said was that I've decided to

stay and would like you to stay too. Otherwise it's a pointless exercise.'

Because he wanted to be here with her.

Ashling felt light-headed.

'Don't you normally stay for the weekend if you're here?'

He shook his head and moved over her on the bed, leaning on his hands. 'No, usually I leave again straight away.'

'Oh.'

'But this time I'm inspired to stay.'

That implied—far too dangerously for Ashling's liking—that he hadn't done this before.

Ashling lay back. Zach loomed over her, bronzed skin tight over taut muscles, more tempting than anything she'd ever known before. She knew that it would be cooler to try and not appear too available, but she was afraid that horse had bolted long ago.

'Well?'

'Okay… I'll stay.'

A bubble of excitement rose up inside her. She reached down and twitched open Zach's towel. It fell from his hips to the bed, exposing every inch of his masculinity.

She met his eye. 'Oops…'

He smiled and came down over her, crushing her deliciously to the bed. '*Oops*, indeed.'

CHAPTER TEN

WHEN ASHLING WOKE again it was much later. A throbbing noise had woken her but she couldn't place it. She was alone in Zach's bedroom and she stretched luxuriously under the sheet, feeling thoroughly decadent.

She got up and put on the sweatpants and T-shirt again to go to her own room, wincing a little as she moved, her muscles aching.

She didn't see anyone on her way. When she got there she looked out of the window and saw that most of the event decorations were already down. The marquee was half dismantled. She realised then that it was after lunch.

She went into her bathroom and looked at herself, eyes widening. Tousled hair, pink cheeks, a little bit of red on her jaw—a slight irritation from Zach's stubble. She almost didn't recognise herself.

She took off his clothes and dived into her shower, before he would come looking for her and find her documenting every bit of evidence of his lovemaking on her body.

When she was out and freshened up she felt slightly less dreamy, a little more in control again. Which she knew would probably last for about a second in Zach's company.

She weakly pushed aside the clamour of her conscience, demanding to know if she had really thought this through. Zach epitomised everything she disdained, and yet all that felt hollow now. It wasn't that black and white. He was a complex man. Surely, she thought a little desperately, she wouldn't be attracted to him if he was driven purely by blind, greedy ambition? Surely she was attracted to him because she saw something more...layers...contradictions.

The realisation that she was trying to justify her decision to stay and indulge in an affair with a man who was entirely wrong for her drove Ashling from her room.

She was wearing the only other piece of clothing she'd brought, not having expected to stay beyond today. It was a yellow sundress, with wide straps over her shoulders and little buttons all the way down the front.

When she got to the reception hall she saw Diana, placing a big vase of blooming flowers on the centre table.

The woman looked up and saw her, smiled. 'You'll be pleased to hear that the chef, Marcel, is fine. They think it was some kind of a panic attack.'

To Ashling's mortification, she realised she'd forgotten about the chef. Zach's form of distraction was too potent. Genuinely relieved, she said, 'That's good news.'

'I believe you and Zach are staying for the rest of the weekend?'

Ashling couldn't help blushing. 'Yes... I hope that doesn't put you out too much?'

The woman smiled wider and said, *sotto voce*, 'Not at all, my dear. I'm delighted to see him actually using the house for once. It's a crying shame to use it as little as he does, and I know he enjoys it here.'

More evidence that this wasn't usual for him, which made Ashling's heart speed up.

Diana said, 'He told me that if I saw you to tell you he's making some calls in his study. You're to have some lunch on the terrace and make yourself at home—he'll come and find you when he's finished.' The housekeeper winked at her. 'If I were you, on a beautiful day like this, I'd use the pool. Or even the lake—it's deep and perfectly safe for swimming.'

The thought of a swim in either the pool or the lake was definitely appealing. But as Diana was walking away Ashling thought of something. 'The Stephanides...do you know where they are? Maybe Elena would like another yoga lesson.'

Diana turned around, 'Oh, they left a little while ago in the helicopter. They were sorry not to see you, but Zach didn't want to disturb you.'

That must have been what had woken her. Their helicopter leaving. Ashling was disappointed not to have been able to say goodbye. She probably wouldn't see them again and she'd liked them.

'Okay, thanks.'

Ashling had a light salad on the terrace. She saw the garden was miraculously almost back to its original state, thanks to the hive of workers clearing everything. Not used to feeling redundant, when she was finished she took her lunch things into the kitchen, but was quickly shooed out by Diana.

She explored the gardens a little more, walked down to the lake. It was utterly idyllic. A beautiful summer's day. Just a small breeze. The water looked seriously tempting. Ashling looked back towards the house. She couldn't see a thing—the foliage shielded the lake from view.

Before she could think about it too much—*'Don't overthink it, hmm?'*—she scowled at Zach's voice intruding in her head and undid the buttons on her dress, letting it drop to the wooden jetty. She slipped off her underwear. She wasn't wearing a bra.

Before she lost her nerve entirely, she dived into the lake.

Zach had looked all over for Ashling. No sign. The last of the event staff were leaving, and he thought of Ashling mentioning getting a lift because she'd assumed he'd meant her to leave so that he could stay here on his own.

It was something he'd never done. Instinctively he'd shied away from owning the space completely. Avoided thinking about what it meant.

He was down at the end of the garden now, near the trees that bordered the lake. He heard a sound.

He walked through the trees and emerged near the jetty. The first thing he saw was a splash of yellow. A discarded dress. He scanned the lake. Then he saw her. She was on her back, floating, her arms outstretched. Limbs pale. The twin mounds of her breasts were visible above the water line…the small pebbles of her nipples. He could see her belly, and the dark blonde cluster of curls that hid the moist and hot evidence of how much she wanted him.

Zach's body jerked in response. He shed his own clothes and executed a near-soundless dive into the water, coming up for air just as Ashling turned her head. She squealed and lost her balance, sinking under the water. Zach reached for her, tugging her up again.

She came up gasping, hair slicked back, her body lithe and smooth. 'What the…? I didn't even hear you…'

Zach pulled her into him and she put her arms around his neck. The sharp points of her breasts against his chest sent blood rushing to his head and groin.

'Put your legs around me.'

She did it wordlessly.

He covered her mouth with his, relishing that sweet, cushiony softness, then giving way to something deeper and more erotic when she opened up to him.

She squirmed in his arms and he reached between them to where she was exposed, sliding his fingers along the slick folds of flesh before exploring deeper, sliding in one finger, then two. She tensed against him and he felt her shudders of release, the contractions around his fingers.

He pulled back. She looked at him, shocked.

'You're so responsive…'

It was beyond gratifying to have this effect on her. Gratifying enough to almost take the edge off his own sharp need. But then the dreamy soft-focus look faded from her face and she reached for him, circling his length with her hand, stroking his flesh until he was the one losing control and shuddering into her hand.

Breathless at the speed with which they'd responded

to each other, Zach didn't try to hold her when she pushed back a little. He watched her tread water, a little bit away. His body felt languorous.

He said, 'If I'd known the lake was this much fun I would have used it long before now.'

Ashling trod water. 'You haven't used it before? But it's amazing. If I lived here I'd never leave and I'd swim here every day.'

Colour poured into her cheek—which was astounding given what they'd just done.

'That is… I don't mean I want to live here. I mean, I would, who wouldn't? But that's not what I—'

Zach took pity on her, reaching for her again, pulling her into his rapidly recovering body. 'Don't over-think it, Ash.'

She rolled her eyes and pushed free of his embrace again. She smiled at him cheekily and said, 'Race you to the jetty.'

'What does the winner get?'

'To have their wicked way with the loser.'

'I thought I just did that?'

Ashling splashed water at him, and then turned and struck out with a graceful crawl to the jetty.

Zach had no problem losing this game. He just watched her, an alien sensation of lightness filling his chest. Then he struck out after her to avoid deciphering what that sensation was.

'I've given Diana and Rob the rest of the weekend off, so they can go and visit their grandkids. Diana has left meals in the fridge, so we won't starve.'

So they were here alone now.

The prospect of that sent more than a tremor of

awareness and anticipation through Ashling. She was still reeling from the aftermath of Zach joining her in the lake a few hours ago. From watching him pull his sleek body out of the water and the fact that he'd revealed that he'd never swum in the lake before.

They'd walked back up to the house, their clothes pulled on over damp bodies. Zach had had to go and make a few calls, and Ashling had taken the opportunity to have another shower and try to gather her wits again. Except she had a feeling that as long as she spent time with Zach any sense of equilibrium or control would be elusive.

She wondered if it would ever come back.

'What would you like to drink?'

Ashling had joined Zach on the terrace for an aperitif. The evening was humid. The sky was turning a bruised colour. 'White wine, please.'

He came out with their drinks. He was wearing dark trousers and a dark polo shirt. He looked vital and sexy.

He observed, 'You like colour, don't you?'

Ashling made a face. 'I had to borrow some more clothes. I didn't bring enough with me for the weekend.'

She wore a strapless black silk jumpsuit, with splashes of vivid colour.

He said, 'It suits you.'

'I didn't always like colour,' Ashling admitted. 'I used to prefer to fade into the background.'

Zach affected a look of shock. 'Not possible.'

Ashling bit back a smile. Like this, he was…irresistible. And she didn't have to resist him.

The thought was heady. Intoxicating.

'Why did you want to fade into the background?' he asked.

Ashling gave a little shrug. 'My mum was a single parent. We were living in a posh area, albeit very much downstairs. My school was conservative. Most other kids had two parents. My mum was…not afraid to express herself. She wore her red hair piled up. Big jewellery. Trendy clothes. And Cassie's dad never let me forget where I belonged.'

'How?'

Ashling told him the story of Cassie's father not allowing her in the main part of the house. 'It's silly, and it was a long time ago, but I still feel intimidated sometimes. Especially in places like this. As if someone is going to come along and accuse me of trespassing.'

She looked at Zach, where he stood near her by the terrace wall. His face was in shadow, which made it easier for her to say, 'That night of the party four years ago… I only realised when I was walking up to you that they'd totally set me up to look as out of place as possible. To make it even worse…for you.'

'But it affected you too?'

'Yes—if that's any consolation.'

'It's in the past now.'

'Is it?' Ashling almost whispered, afraid to ask. 'Am I still being punished?'

Zach put his glass down and took hers, setting it aside. He came close and cupped her face in his hands. Ashling felt vulnerable. There were moments like these when she felt so exposed, and it would take nothing much at all for Zach to capitalise on her vulnerability and crush her. She held her breath.

He said, 'No more punishment. Now it's just about pleasure.'

Ashling released her breath, shakily, and it mingled with Zach's as he covered her mouth with his and showed her exactly the difference between punishment and pleasure.

To say that Ashling felt as if she was in a bubble outside of time was an understatement. She lay on a sunbed in a swimsuit she'd borrowed from the pool house and wasn't even sure what time of day it was, never mind what day.

The last twenty-four hours had been spent mainly in bed, punctuated by trips to the kitchen. And once to the lake again, as dawn had risen. That swim had been magical…magical enough to make Ashling very afraid that she was fast losing any grip on remembering what this weekend was about.

Short and hot.

Weakly, she felt she could happily live in this dreamlike state and never go back to the real world again. She'd never felt so at peace. Which was disconcerting when she was in a milieu that she'd always found a little uncomfortable.

She heard the sound of someone emerging from the pool and opened her eyes, squinting up at a six-footplus embodiment of masculine perfection, with water sluicing down over his hard muscles. Short swimtrunks left little to the imagination.

'Sure you don't want to swim?'

Ashling feigned a level of nonchalance she really wasn't feeling. 'I'm happy to take in the view.'

She squealed when he came down over her, showering her with droplets of water. This relaxed version of Zach Temple was more than a revelation. He was fatally seductive.

He kissed her, and any hope of pretending to be nonchalant melted. The craving he woke in her with just a look, a kiss, was seriously addictive. Ashling had heard people talk about sex as if it was a drug and she'd never understood it. Till now...

When Zach pulled back she went with him, loath to break the contact. He lay down on the sunbed beside hers.

Ashling turned on her side to look at him. 'This house must have been amazing for a child.'

'I'm sure it was,' Zach said lazily.

Ashling was surprised. 'It wasn't in your family?'

He shook his head, eyes closed. 'I bought it a few years ago.'

Ashling recalled what he'd said about his father. 'You said your father's not in your life...were your parents divorced?'

For a long moment Zach said nothing, and then, 'My mother was a single parent. I grew up in a tower block in one of the roughest parts of London.'

It took a long moment for that to sink in. When it did, Ashling sat up on the sunbed, shocked.

Zach turned his head and looked at her. Mocking. 'Weren't expecting that, were you?'

No. Not in a million years. She was speechless as she absorbed this. Finally she said faintly, 'But you went to boarding school... Oxbridge...'

'Scholarships.'

Suddenly Ashling felt cold, in spite of the heat. 'Your father...'

'He wanted nothing to do with me. He has his own family, who were all bred with the right woman.'

This was all too sickeningly familiar. 'You have half-siblings?'

'Yes.'

Ashling wrapped her arms around her knees. 'I just assumed you came from that world.'

'Rich. Entitled.' He stated the words.

She nodded. Zach was expressionless, but she could see the tension in his form. She felt defensive, because she hated it that she'd misjudged him so badly. 'You let me assume...'

He shrugged. 'I find that people don't really like to have their assumptions disproved.'

That hurt. But he was right.

She said, 'I pride myself on not judging people, but I judged you.'

Because it had kept him at arm's length.

'You saw what you wanted to see.'

Ashling swung her legs around to the side of the sunbed. She felt agitated. 'Zach...we've had the same experience. More or less.'

'It's a small world.'

He sounded blasé, but Ashling wasn't fooled. 'Have you ever met your father?'

Zach sat up and reached for her, tugging her up from her sunbed and over to his. She landed in an inelegant sprawl across his chest, her breasts crushed against warm, damp skin.

He said, 'Funnily enough, I can think of better things to do than talk about my father.'

He trailed his hands up along her waist, across the bare skin of her back, and then traced the side of her breast, exposed by the far too daringly cut swimsuit that she hadn't been able to resist choosing earlier. Now she regretted it.

He took his hands away and looked at her. 'But if you'd prefer to talk…'

Ashling wanted to scowl. He knew exactly how he affected her. The inevitable fire lit up her blood and turned it molten in seconds. And she of all people could understand his need to deflect.

What he'd just revealed was huge. Maybe she wasn't ready to pursue that line of conversation either…afraid of what it would change between them.

Weakly, she put her hands on either side of his head, and just before touching her mouth to his she said, 'You win… I vote we go with this…'

'You don't have to cook.'

'I like cooking. Just sit there and look pretty.'

Ashling pushed a glass of wine towards Zach, who was sitting on the other side of the island. What she didn't mention was that she found cooking therapeutic—especially when she needed to think stuff over in her head. Like the bombshell Zach had dropped earlier about his background…

He'd managed to keep her pretty distracted for the rest of the afternoon, until she'd left him sleeping in bed, had a shower and come downstairs. She'd been inspired to cook when she'd seen Diana's well-stocked larder and fridge.

The fly in the ointment was that the object of her ruminations was sitting a few feet away, looking far too distracting in a dark T-shirt. She didn't have to see his bottom half, because the image of him appearing in the kitchen in worn denims a short time before was seared on to her brain.

'What are you cooking?'

'Seafood risotto.'

'Tell me how you ended up doing a cordon bleu course.'

Ashling added onion, garlic and some other ingredients to a heavy pan. 'It was the year my mother took me to Paris for my birthday.'

'You were eighteen.'

Ashling looked at him, hating the spurt of warmth in her chest because he remembered. 'Yes. Well, I fell in love with the food, so when I'd saved up enough money to do a basic course I went back. I waitressed to make money while doing it.'

Zach took a sip of wine. 'So why didn't you become a chef?'

Ashling added rice to the pan, stirring with a wooden spoon. 'I knew from early on that I wasn't really cut out to be a chef. I don't have the temperament.'

'You're too nice.'

Ashling smiled sweetly and added white wine to the mixture, and more stock. She'd found a white off-the-shoulder peasant-style dress in the dressing room. She was aware of Zach's eyes on her, but she was still not quite believing that she could be that enticing to him.

Short and hot. That was why. Tomorrow was Monday. They'd go back to London...and that would be that.

'Did you ever meet *your* father?'

Zach's question took her off-guard. She looked at him, and deflected for a moment by saying, 'It's okay for you to ask me, but not for me to ask you?'

He was unrepentant. 'Absolutely.'

Ashling hated talking about her father. Even though her mother had done her best to try and help Ashling not to feel bitter about him. But bitterness and anger at being rejected lingered. Especially after that last time.

'I've met him three times. When I was four—too young to really remember much, except him and my mother fighting. And then when I was nine. It was a disaster.'

'Why?'

Ashling focused on stirring the rice. 'He took me to an expensive toyshop and couldn't understand why I wouldn't pick a toy. I wanted to talk to him, but he just wanted to fob me off with *stuff*. I wasn't into toys. He didn't understand me—I'd worn a bright red dress and he made a comment about me attracting attention. He was probably terrified someone would recognise him. And I cried because I'd made him angry, attracting even more attention. For years after that I refused to wear anything too bright or outlandish, because I thought if I faded into the background then he might come back…give me another chance.'

'And now you wear bright colours to show him you don't care?'

Emotion at Zach's far too incisive remark almost closed Ashling's throat. When she felt she could speak again she said lightly, 'Maybe you should have gone into therapy. You could give my mother a run for her money.'

'You said there were three times you'd met him. What was the third?'

Ashling wanted to scowl at Zach, but she was afraid of the emotion bubbling under the surface. 'The third

time wasn't long before that night…*the* night…' She
sneaked him a look.

He raised a brow, 'Go on.'

'I was at the theatre with Cassie and I saw him in
the crowd. I got such a shock. I acted without thinking.
Cassie tried to stop me, but I went over and tapped him
on the shoulder. He didn't even recognise me. I had to
tell him who I was.'

Ashling rubbed her arm as if she could still feel the
pain of his hand gripping her, hauling her to one side.

'What happened?'

Again, Ashling forced a lightness into her voice that
she wasn't feeling. 'Let's just say that he made it clear I
wasn't welcome in his milieu. I hadn't realised it, but he
was with his family. He was afraid I'd cause a scene.'

Zach sounded disgusted. '*His* milieu? You had as
much of a right to be there as he did.'

'That's what Cassie said.'

'Some people aren't fit to be parents.' Zach's tone
was stark.

Ashling forced a smile, wanting to banish the toxic
memories. 'My mum is amazing. I'm lucky to have
her. What was your mum like?'

Zach got up and took his glass to stand at the open
French doors that led out to a kitchen garden full of
plants and herbs. Ashling could still smell the thyme
she'd picked earlier for the risotto.

She thought for a second that he was going to ignore
her, but then he said, 'She was driven.'

Ashling carefully added the prepared seafood to the
rice mixture. 'What do you mean? She was ambitious?'

Zach let out a short, harsh laugh. 'No! As she liked

to tell me often, she didn't have the luxury of being ambitious because she was a single parent.'

Ashling's heart clenched. She'd witnessed how tough it was for single parents. 'She couldn't afford to get qualifications?'

'She was intelligent. Intelligent enough to get a place at university. She would have been the first in her family. She came from a working-class town in the north of England. She had plans to go. She was working three different jobs to make enough money. That's how she met my father. She was a cleaner at the House of Commons.'

Ashling stopped stirring the risotto. 'Your father is a politician?'

'He's retired now. A peer of the realm.' The sneer in Zach's voice was unmistakable.

Ashling put down the spoon. 'That's why he didn't want anything to do with you?'

'He didn't want an illegitimate child messing up his very public life. He gave my mother money to get rid of me, but she was too proud. She sent the money back to him, told him she'd be keeping me.'

The risotto started hissing, Ashling stirred it again.

Zach said, 'I grew up very aware of the fact that I had to justify my existence. To prove myself. To pay her back for her sacrifice. She didn't have a life because of me.'

Ashling bit her lip. Then she said, 'You were her life. She must have been so proud of you.'

Zach's mouth compressed. 'I don't think she ever saw much past the fact that I'd sent my father a message that I'd thrived in spite of his rejection. That he hadn't broken her with his treatment of her. She was obsessed with the fact that I'd succeeded enough to be accepted into his world. My "rightful world", according to her.'

'Did you ever meet him?'

Zach walked away from the open door and put his glass of wine down on the island. He avoided her eyes.

It was so unlike him not to look her in the eye that she said, 'Zach...?'

He looked at her. She couldn't read the expression on his face, but something sent a shiver down her spine.

He said, 'We've moved in the same circles for some time now...we tend to avoid each other.'

'But...' Ashling trailed off as something occurred to her. She felt sick. 'He was there that night, wasn't he? Four years ago? He was there and he saw the whole thing and...' Ashling stopped stirring and sat on a stool, feeling weak at the thought.

Zach nodded. Grim. 'He wasn't just there—he was the one who set me up.'

She looked at Zach, horrified. But it made a kind of sick sense. Humiliate your illegitimate son to send him a lesson. And she'd played a role in that lesson.

Ashling shook her head, 'Zach, I'm so sorry. I had no idea.'

'How could you? I only found out after the fact. If I'd seriously suspected that you knew any of this we wouldn't be having this conversation.'

A smell of burning tickled Ashling's nostrils. She gave a gasp of dismay and turned off the heat, reaching for the pan handle before stopping to think.

The pain of the burn registered at about the same time as Zach moved like lightning and had her hand under the running cold water tap.

'It's fine...honestly.'

But Zach kept her hand there, numbing the pain.

Emotion welled inside Ashling before she could stop it. Emotion at the thought of Zach overcoming serious adversity to achieve above and beyond what anyone could have imagined. The thought of his mother…giving up her life for her son, but also sending him a toxic message about revenge and retribution.

And Ashling's own part in it all. And, even worse, her quick and easy judgement of him. Assuming the worst. Because it had been easier than believing things might be more complex—that he might be more complex. Because that would make him…so dangerous.

He turned off the water and wrapped Ashling's palm in a damp towel. She was embarrassed now, and feeling intensely vulnerable. 'That's really not necessary.'

He tipped up her chin. She blinked back the emotion, drowning in his dark eyes. She had no defences left.

His mouth quirked. 'See what happens when we talk? It's dangerous.'

She smiled, but it felt wobbly. And then Zach led her over to the dining table and sat her down. He went back over to the stove, dumped the burnt risotto in the bin, making Ashling wince, and then she watched, fascinated, as he tied an apron over his jeans and expertly rustled up a fluffy cheese and mushroom omelette served with warm crusty bread and wine.

By the time he sat down she was very afraid that the revelations of the evening and Zach's easy charm had left her no place to hide from the truth. The truth that she was falling in love with him. With a man who had just told her in no uncertain terms that he might come from her world, but he had no intention of going back there again.

And she couldn't even blame him, after what he'd told her.

CHAPTER ELEVEN

THE FOLLOWING MORNING Ashling made an unintelligible grunting sound at the persistent calling of her name. She felt so deliciously lethargic and relaxed, and she squealed when the sheet was ripped off her body, leaving her naked and exposed. The fact that the culprit was very much responsible for her exposed and naked state wasn't much comfort.

Zach was standing at the end of the bed in jeans and a long-sleeved polo shirt, hair damp from a shower. 'Come on.'

Ashling squinted. 'It's not even light outside.' A thought struck her. Her heart sank. 'We're leaving for London already?'

Zach must have early meetings lined up.

But he said, 'Not quite yet. We're doing something first.'

He pointed to the end of the bed. 'I've laid out some clothes. Get dressed and meet me downstairs in fifteen minutes.'

Ashling came up on one elbow. 'Where are we going?'

'You'll see. Hurry up.'

Ashling hauled herself out of bed and had a quick

shower, relishing the smell of Zach's spicy gel. Wrapped in a towel, she looked at the clothes he'd laid out. They were from the dressing room. Jeans and a stripy Breton top...sneakers.

Ashling got dressed and went downstairs. Zach greeted her with a cup of coffee and a croissant. He said, 'I'll be outside when you're ready.'

Intrigued, Ashling gulped down some coffee and a couple of bites of croissant, then went outside—and nearly tripped over her own feet. Zach was shrugging on a leather jacket and standing beside a beast of a motorbike. Dawn was just starting to appear in the sky.

He handed her a leather jacket. 'It's probably a bit big, but it'll do.'

Ashling took it. She was wide awake now, and speechless. She'd imagined Zach on a motorbike, but nothing could have prepared her for the reality when he zipped up the jacket and swung a leg over to straddle the machine.

He handed her a helmet and showed her where to step to help her hitch a leg over so she could sit behind him. She put a hand on his shoulder. When she was behind him her body naturally slid down right behind his. Her pelvis tucked against his backside. She automatically put her hands around his waist.

He put a hand on her thigh and turned to look at her, straightened her helmet. 'Okay?'

She nodded. She was exhilarated, and they hadn't even started moving yet. He started the bike and the engine roared to life underneath her. Between her legs where she was still tender.

They drove out of the estate and onto the empty main road. As Zach drove the sky lightened more and more. Ashling felt as if they were the only people in the world.

After about fifteen minutes Zach drove the bike through a gate where there was a huge hangar and a small plane in a huge field. He stopped the bike. They got off. He took off her helmet. She felt a little wobbly after the adrenalin of the bike-ride. He took her hand and led her over to where a man was waiting by the plane. Zach introduced him as the tow pilot.

Ashling was beginning to wonder if this was a dream. 'Tow pilot?'

Zach took her around to the other side of the plane, where she saw the most delicate flimsy-looking glider.

She looked from it to Zach. 'No way…'

He said, 'Do you trust me?'

Ashling wished she didn't. She wished she still had some tiny bit of distrust left. But he'd eroded it. The problem was that she didn't believe for a second that he trusted *her*. He wanted her. But that was it. And today they'd go back to London and this would be over.

Short and hot and over.

She nodded. 'Yes—yes, I do.' He didn't have to know that she meant it in a deeper sense. That she trusted him with her life. *With her heart.*

He helped her into the glider. which looked like a toy. She sat in the back seat and he got into the front. She watched, struck dumb, as the tow pilot got into the small plane and another man did something with the rope attached to their glider.

Then the other plane was moving, tugging their glider plane along behind it, and then suddenly they were off the ground, soaring into the sky behind the plane. And then the rope must have been detached, because the plane was banking left and they were going straight on, gliding higher and higher.

The thing that struck Ashling was the silence. All she could hear was the pounding of her heart. She was too afraid to move for a moment, and then she took in her surroundings, the countryside around them, as dawn broke over the horizon bathing everything pink and golden.

'Okay?' Zach half turned his head.

Euphoria gripped Ashling as the shock of what they were doing wore off. She nodded, emotion gripping her throat. 'Yes—yes! It's amazing.'

It was like nothing she'd ever experienced. Transcendental.

Ashling had no idea how long they stayed in the air…only that she would have happily stayed up there for ever.

When they got back to the field and landed, Ashling was mortified to find tears on her cheeks. She quickly wiped at them as Zach undid his seatbelt and got out.

He turned around and reached for her. He saw her face and frowned. 'Hey, are you okay?'

Ashling nodded and stood beside him on rubbery legs. Lingering emotion made her voice husky. 'I've never experienced anything like that…it was beautiful. Thank you.'

She reached up and put her mouth to his jaw. Disconcertingly, she was reminded of that fateful night, of kissing him in the same spot. Zach pulled back. A shiver of foreboding went down her spine. She told herself she was being ridiculous. Paranoid.

After a quick chat with the pilots who ran the company, Zach led her back over to the motorbike. She couldn't explain it, but something had shifted between them since they'd landed. Zach didn't meet her eye as he put on her helmet, made sure she was secure. His touch was brisk. Impersonal.

She clung to him on the way back to the house, but she couldn't escape the feeling that Zach was regretting that impetuous move.

It had been impossibly romantic. And this wasn't about romance.

In the end, no amount of premonition could have warned Ashling just how brutally efficient Zach could be when dispensing with a lover.

The beautiful glider experience had obviously been a goodbye gift. As soon as they'd got back to the house Zach had turned distant in a way that he hadn't been since that night four years ago. Because since she'd met him again he'd been far too vengeful to be distant and then…then it had turned into something else.

Diana had been back at the house when they'd returned from their glider experience. Had it been Ashling's imagination or had she taken one look at Zach and Ashling and then looked at Ashling with sympathy? As if she had intuited exactly what was happening.

Zach had said, 'We'll be leaving within the hour. You should pack and get ready.'

And now they were in the back of his chauffeur driven car returning to London. No helicopter this time. Zach was in a three-piece suit. Ashling was in the laundered clothes she'd worn on her arrival.

He was on his phone now, speaking in French. It made her think of how far he'd come. From nothing. And how much it must mean to him to be considered equal by his peers and, more importantly, his father who'd rejected him.

To her surprise she felt her phone vibrate in her bag. She took it out. It was just a random text from her phone provider about billing. She read the last text exchange she'd had with Cassie over the weekend, when she'd last checked her phone.

Cassie had been wondering how she was, and Ashling—feeling inordinately guilty—had mentioned something vague about doing errands for Zach while Gwen was still away. Cassie had rung her then, and Ashling had tried to ascertain what was going on with Luke, the guy she was sleeping with, but her friend had been unusually elusive.

But then, Ashling hadn't been able to speak either, and she'd been equally elusive about what was really going on with her and Zach. She longed to talk to her friend now, though. But she'd have to wait.

Cassie would be back soon. Order would be restored.

For Zach, it would be as if nothing had happened—except for the fact that he'd settled an old score.

For Ashling, though... She couldn't even go there.

'I can get the tube.'

'Gerard will drop you home. No argument.'

The driver caught Ashling's eye in the mirror. 'No problem, miss.'

Weakly, Ashling smiled, 'Thanks, Gerard.'

They were almost at Zach's Mayfair townhouse. The city looked busy and intimidating to Ashling after the last few days in a bucolic paradise. She felt as if a layer of skin had been removed.

Zach pushed a button and the privacy partition went up between them and Gerard. He turned to her. She noticed that he must have shaved since they'd taken the glider flight that morning. It struck her then, in a moment of insight, that Zach must love the rush of adrenalin because he'd had to be so careful for his whole life not to make waves. To succeed and excel.

The fact that she'd recognised that only made this moment even harder.

She spoke first, to stall whatever it was he was going to say. 'Thank you… This morning was amazing. The whole weekend…'

'Thank you for being there. The deal with Georgios Stephanides… I don't know if it would have happened without you.'

'I'm sure that's not true, but it was the least I could do, considering the destruction I caused in the past.'

He shook his head. 'That's in the past. Gone.'

The car pulled to a stop outside Zach's house. He said, 'Look, Ashling, this was—'

She put up a hand, her chest tight. 'You really don't have to say anything, Zach. We both know what this is. Was. It's cool.'

If he mentioned *short and hot* she might hit him.

His jaw was tight. Eventually he said, 'After this morning I was afraid that—'

Ashling shook her head so forcibly she was afraid it might fall off. 'No. It was lovely—and thank you again. Now I should really get going. I have tons to catch up on.'

'Of course. Goodbye, Ashling.'

'Bye, Zach.'

He got out of the car, took a bag out of the boot,

and Ashling watched him go up the steps to the house. The door opened before he reached it and she caught a glimpse of the taciturn Peters.

Vengeance meted out. Order restored. Interlude over.

Ashling was glad the driver left the privacy partition up for the duration of the journey back to her and Cassie's apartment. Because she cried like a baby the whole way.

Zach lasted until lunchtime.

He'd thought he was doing the right thing. Seeing Ashling's tears that morning had been the biggest wake-up call of his life. They'd reminded him of the emotion he'd seen in her eyes the previous evening, when he'd all but spilled every gut he had at her feet. And her too. When she'd told him about her father he'd felt violent.

And had that made him run? Or send her packing? No, they'd eaten, drunk wine, made love. And then he'd woken her up this morning and taken her out on a glider—one of the most transcendental experiences of his life, shared with no one else before.

What the hell are you doing?

The words had resounded in his head like a klaxon when he'd seen her tears. In that split second he'd realised how far off-track the weekend had veered. At what point had *short and hot* turned into deep and meaningful?

An image formed in Zach's head. Heat pulsed into his blood.

It had happened right about when he'd found Ashling floating in his lake like a sexy water nymph.

He still wanted her.

It had taken all his restraint not to kiss her in the car. But she'd been looking at him with those huge eyes. Full of an emotion that convinced him he was doing the right thing.

But maybe he'd underestimated her. After all, she'd had a couple of relationships. She was savvy. Smart. Maybe he was doing them both a disservice by ending things so abruptly...

He assured himself that he was moving on to the next chapter of his life, and that he'd never been clearer about where he wanted to go—thanks in a large part to the person who had almost helped derail it four years ago.

But maybe the next chapter didn't have to start today.

Ashling had put on a pair of old cut-off shorts and a crocheted wrap-over top. She was attempting to take her mind off things by doing a bit of gardening in the small patch she and Cassie had outside their apartment at the back. But it wasn't doing much to ease the ache in her chest.

When the door buzzer rang she welcomed the distraction, dusting off her hands. Expecting to see her neighbour, or a delivery person, Ashling opened the door and blinked stupidly up at Zachary Temple.

He was halfway through saying something but Ashling was already in his arms, legs around his waist, mouth clamped to his. He walked them back into her apartment and kicked the door shut behind him.

Much later, in Ashling's bed, with the sounds of children playing on the street outside and sirens in the distance, they had a conversation.

Zach. 'This doesn't mean…'

Ashling.'I know.'

'What we said at the start—'

'What *you* said.'

'That this would be—'

'*Don't* say it now. It doesn't need to be said again. I know what this is.'

'You do?'

'Yes. And that's okay.' *Liar.*

'Okay. Good.'

'Good.'

'We're clear…?'

Ashling turned to Zach in the bed and twined her bare legs with his, relishing the feel of his body responding to hers. 'Clear as crystal.'

She kissed him then, to stop him saying anything else. She didn't need to be reminded of her weakness. Or that this was just a stay of execution.

Thirty-six hours later Ashling was on the other side of London in Zach's townhouse. She adjusted the pearl-encrusted collar that tied at the back of her neck. The dress was sleeveless, held up by the collar, with a line of pearls running from the collar on either side of the edge of the bodice of the dress, under her arms and around to the back. The rest of the dress was black, with a nipped-in waist, and it fell to the floor in a single elegant fall of material.

It was classic and…conservative. Her overriding instinct was to add a bit of colour. But she told herself it wasn't appropriate.

She'd come to Zach's house yesterday, after he'd spent the day and the night at her apartment. She hadn't expected anything social. But he'd asked her to come to a charity event this evening.

She'd said, 'Is that a good idea? People might start to ask questions…wonder who I am…'

Cassie, for starters. Her friend was due to arrive home any day now, and Ashling had no idea how she was going to begin explaining what had happened.

But Zach had brushed it off. 'It's a private event… tight security. It shouldn't attract too much attention.'

Then she'd said, 'I don't have anything to wear to an event.'

He'd said, 'Leave it with me. I'll arrange it.'

And this was the dress that had been delivered. Obviously to his specifications.

She'd put her hair up, to try and look as sophisticated as the dress.

Zach appeared in the doorway, wearing a tuxedo and carrying a box. He said, 'You look…stunning.'

A part of Ashling was a little disappointed with Zach's obvious approval. Especially after what he'd intuited the other night at his country house—that she wore colour to rebel against her father's lack of interest. It might have started like that, but now it was her. Who she was. Her essence.

Right now, though, she didn't really feel like *her*. Not like she had in that glorious dress at the weekend. She felt she was betraying herself a little.

But then she told herself she was being ridiculous. It was one night. One dress. These moments with Zach were finite.

'Thank you.' She affected a little curtsey.

Zach came into the room and opened the box, saying, 'I thought you might need something to go with the dress.'

Ashling looked inside and gasped. There was a pearl bracelet, with what looked like a diamond catch, and pearl drop earrings.

She looked at Zach. 'Are these real?'

'Of course.'

Ashling shook her head. 'Zach, I can't. They're too valuable. What if I lose an earring or the bracelet falls—?'

'They're yours. A gift.'

Her mouth dropped. A veritable tsunami of conflicting emotions swirled in her belly. When she could move her jaw again she said, 'I can't…really. It's too much.'

But Zach was already taking out the bracelet and fastening it around her wrist, saying, 'Just try them on, hmm…?'

He handed her the earrings. She wasn't even sure why she was so reluctant, or why there was a feeling of gathering dread in her belly, so she put them on. They swung from her ears, their lustrous sheen catching the light.

Zach put his hands on her shoulders. He towered above her. They matched. Her black dress and pearls with his classic black and white tuxedo. And yet something jarred inside Ashling.

But then he was taking her hand and leading her out, downstairs to his car. They passed Peters on the way, and if Ashling wasn't mistaken the man gave her a sliver of a smile.

Now she was even more freaked out.

* * *

It took Zach a minute to realise why he couldn't find Ashling in the crowd. Because she looked like everyone else in their tones of black, grey, white and not many variations on those themes.

He pushed aside the niggle of his conscience. He'd deliberately instructed the boutique to deliver a dress that he knew Ashling wouldn't choose for herself. Obeying some very nebulous desire to see her in another environment. *His* environment. Because he needed to know if—

'Sorry. I got lost coming back from the ladies.'

Zach looked at Ashling. His eye was drawn to the splash of colour just above one ear. Delicate pink flowers tucked artfully into her hair.

'What's that?'

She touched the flowers. 'Is it too much? I spotted the hotel florists changing the flower display. They were going to end up in a bin, so I took a few.'

Zach shook his head, biting back a smile. 'No, it's not too much. It's pretty.'

He took her hand, feeling something inside him ease—just before he looked across the room and saw something, *someone*, and any sense of ease dissolved in a rush of hot emotion.

'What is it?' Ashling had clearly noticed the change in him immediately.

'My father.' He bit the words out.

He barely heard Ashling's intake of breath or felt her hand tightening around his.

'Where is he?'

'Talking to his wife. The mother of my half-brothers and sisters.'

* * *

Ashling followed Zach's eyeline to a tall man in the crowd. Distinguished. The woman beside him was also tall and elegant. The perfect couple. Ashling felt sick for Zach. She could imagine only too well how he must be feeling. Betrayed and rejected all over again.

A surge of protectiveness rose up inside her—and a need to right the wrong she'd done four years before. Zach's father had used her as an unwitting tool to hurt his own son.

Before she could think it through, Ashling had pulled her hand free of Zach's and was marching through the crowd towards his father, borne aloft on a wave of righteous anger.

She wasn't even aware of the sense of déjà-vu: walking through a crowd towards a tall man…walking around to stand in front of him.

This time she wasn't nervous, though. She was livid.

Zach's father looked her up and down. His eyes were blue. Not dark. Cold.

'Yes? Can I help you?'

'Don't you recognise me?'

The man immediately looked discomfited and guilty, more than hinting at a lifetime of behaviour similar to what he'd subjected Zach's mother to.

Ashling was disgusted. 'No, I don't mean like that. I mean from four years ago, when you hired an actor to publicly humiliate your own son.'

The man's eyes narrowed and comprehension dawned. 'You had red hair. A short dress.'

'So you do remember?'

He hissed at her. 'Get out of here now or I'll call the police.'

The women beside him spoke sharply. 'Henry, what is going on?'

The man looked at Ashling, up and down. 'Nothing, darling. This tart is just some opportunist. She shouldn't be here.'

Those words made a red mist descend over Ashling's vision. Her voice rang out. 'Zachary Temple is more of a son than you could ever deserve. You're not fit to clean his shoes. You're a disgrace.'

Before Ashling knew what was happening Zach's father had lifted his hand, as if to strike her, but someone stood in front of her before he could.

Zach. His voice was ice-cold. 'Don't even think about it. I'll have you flat on your back with a broken jaw and the police will be here so quickly your head will be spinning for a year.'

Ashling took a step to the side, to see Zach's father's hand still raised. The look in his eyes was one of pure and utter hatred. His face was mottled. There was a deadly silence. And then a flash of light.

Zach turned, took Ashling's hand, and then everything was a blur until they were outside the venue and Zach was bundling her into the back of his car. Ashling realised she was trembling all over from the overload of adrenalin and emotion. She could still feel herself flinching in anticipation of a physical blow.

Zach was like a statue next to her. The journey back to his house was made in tense silence. As the shock wore off, though, dread settled in Ashling's belly. She'd overstepped the mark—spectacularly. He'd never forgive her for this.

When they got back to the house Zach went straight

into the reception room. Ashling followed him. He poured himself a drink and threw it back.

He turned around. 'What the hell were you thinking, Ashling?'

She swallowed. 'I'm sorry. I just… I saw him and I got so angry when I thought of everything…'

Zach started to pace. 'He could have hurt you. He nearly did!'

Ashling almost flinched again at the memory. 'You stopped him.'

Zach kept pacing. 'Four years ago was bad. It was embarrassing and it cost me. But I managed to overcome the talk and the reputational damage. I worked hard to restore confidence and faith. But now… I have so much more to lose.' He stopped, looked at Ashling. 'The one thing I had going for me was the fact that no one knew who my father was. There were rumours, but that was all. At first I hated it that he didn't acknowledge me. Then I didn't want to be associated with him. But now that's all gone. It'll be all over the papers that I'm Henry Field's son. There'll be constant speculation as to whether or not he influenced my success in any way. My reputation will come under scrutiny all over again.' Zach gestured to Ashling. 'You might look the part this evening, but you've just proved that you really don't belong in this world.'

If he'd slapped her across the face it wouldn't have had the same impact. He might as well have taken out a knife and sliced her heart wide open.

Ashling couldn't breathe for a long moment, so sharp was the pain. Then she said shakily, 'I knew it. You got this dress on purpose, to try and see if I could fit in. Was it some kind of an audition to see if I was suitable for a wider public audience?'

'Well, if it was, you failed.'

Ashling shook her head. 'I didn't ask for this, Zach. I thought we were done.'

He closed the distance between them so fast, she took a step back.

'Don't make me prove you a liar, Ashling. When I turned up at your door you were with me all the way.'

She really didn't need to be reminded of the relief she'd felt right now. 'I meant I didn't ask to be a part of your world. I know it would never work.'

Zach made a rude sound. 'The innocent ingénue is back, I see.'

'What's that supposed to mean?'

'Elena Stephanides has been in touch, looking for your contact details. Apparently you were discussing her investing in a business, the setting up of a yoga studio?'

Ashling's mind was blank for a moment—and then she remembered. It had been a very innocent conversation that she'd passed off as nonsense at the time. Flattered but embarrassed.

She shook her head. 'That was nothing. *Is* nothing. She was complimentary about my yoga teaching. I told her I had a pipedream to one day own my own studio... I had no idea she'd actually follow up on it.'

Zach made another sound. 'Kind of convenient to have a conversation about *"nothing"* with one of the wealthiest women in Europe, though.'

The pain deepened and spread throughout Ashling's body, turning her blood cold. 'I knew you were cynical, Zach, but that is...beyond...'

Zach tugged at his bow-tie, undid his top button. Even now, in the midst of all this, Ashling could still be aware of him. Those long fingers.

'It's not cynical. It's how the world works.'

'Your world. Not mine.'

Zach took down his hand, leaving the bow-tie rakishly undone. 'Oh, yes—because your world is so much more worthy. Because you get enjoyment out of earthy, basic pleasures. Because you're not corrupted by ambition and success and wealth.'

Before she could respond he went on.

'And yet you took to the billionaire lifestyle without too much of a struggle.' He put his hands out, 'Now that we know where we both stand, maybe we can revisit that audition to be my mistress. After all, I don't think we're quite done, are we?'

Ashling was so angry and hurt she was dizzy with it. 'Whatever I felt for you is dead, Zach. I could never want someone so cruel, so cynical—'

She was in his arms and his mouth was on hers before she had time to take another breath.

Ashling managed to resist for about one second, while the anger raged, but then Zach's mouth softened, his arm relaxed infinitesimally, and desire overtook the rage, blazing up in a storm of want and need and hurt and anger. Because even in the midst of her pain she understood his.

Her arms climbed around his neck, her body straining against his, and then he pulled back. He put his hands on her arms, held her away from him. She could feel her hair unravelling. The flowers lay at her feet, wilted. Mocking.

She pulled back too, with a jerky move. 'I think we are done, actually. Goodbye, Zach.'

Ashling turned and walked from the room on very wobbly legs. She went upstairs, changed into her own clothes. Left the dress and the jewellery behind.

This time when she went downstairs there was no disapproving Peters, no sign of Zach.

She opened the door and walked to the nearest tube station and went home.

Zach heard the front door opening and closing. He knew she was gone.

It was only now that the volatile mix of inarticulate rage and lust was finally clearing from his brain. Except when he thought of seeing his father raise his hand to strike Ashling he felt the anger rise again. Not even anger. Murderous rage.

His insides turned to ice. *No.* Not going there.

And then all he could see was Ashling standing in front of him just now. Looking pale. Stricken. Mouth swollen from his kiss. He'd had to put her away from him. He'd been afraid that he wouldn't be able to stop kissing her, and that was all he had intended. To make a point. It had been very important not to expose himself.

There was a bitter taste in his mouth. Four years ago he'd stood in a room and felt the judgement and condemnation of his peers. He'd thought he might never recover. It had happened again this evening. With possibly worse repercussions. He had more to lose now. A lot more.

But instead of *that* being his focus all he could feel were the four walls of the empty room closing in around him and the sensation that, whatever damage had been done in that ballroom full of his peers this evening, somehow the real damage had been done here in this room.

And then he told himself he was being ridiculous. The only damage he needed to worry about was damage limitation. Putting Ashling out of his head once and for all. She was right—they were done. He didn't need a lover who tied him up in so many knots he couldn't think straight. Or a lover who waded in to fight battles he'd been fighting on his own for years.

He didn't need any of that.

He didn't need her.

He didn't need anyone.

In a bid to prove something to himself, Zach went upstairs, taking the stairs two at a time. He found the dress Ashling had been wearing hanging up in the wardrobe. Something about that detail irritated him intensely.

And then he looked around for the sheen of cool, pale pearls. He saw the box and picked it up, opening it. It was empty.

Annoyingly, his first reaction wasn't a sense of vindication because she'd taken the jewellery—after all, he'd told her it was a gift. But he was disappointed.

He was almost out of the room before something caught the corner of his eye. He stopped. The bracelet and earrings were on the top of a chest of drawers, neatly lined up. She hadn't taken them.

CHAPTER TWELVE

THREE DAYS LATER, and back in his office, Zach was in a foul humour. Suddenly he became aware of a commotion coming from the other side of his door and heard Gwen's slightly raised voice.

Zach's heart thumped. *Could it—?*

But before he could finish that thought the door burst open and a man strode in. He looked vaguely familiar, but Zach couldn't place him.

Before he could say anything, the man said, 'I need to know where Cassandra James is.'

'Who the hell are you and how did you get into my office?' Zach shouted to Gwen. "Gwen, get in here."

Gwen appeared at the door, looking concerned. 'I'm so sorry, Mr Temple. He said he had an appointment.'

'Like hell he—'

'I'm Luke Broussard of Broussard Tech.'

Now Zach recognised him. This was the man he'd sent Cassie to suss out in America. He felt anger that it wasn't Ashling—that he'd even wanted it to be *her*—but he cut off that direction of thinking. Focused on the other very valid reason for his anger.

He narrowed his gaze on the man in front of him, who almost as tall as he was. 'Terrific. The man who managed to lose me the best executive assistant I've ever had. What are you doing here? Have you come to gloat?'

'What do you mean "lose you"? Where is Cassandra?'

'I expect she's at home, being head-hunted by one of my rivals. So thanks for that.'

'She's resigned?'

Broussard looked genuinely shocked.

Then he said, 'You need to give me her address. Please, man, I need to talk to her… To explain.'

Zach put up a hand. 'What the hell makes you think I'd give you my executive assistant's address? Why should I? Not only is it unethical, but it's also quite possibly illegal. And I really could not care less if—'

'Because…' the man cut him off, and stopped.

Zach was getting seriously irritated now. 'Because *what*?'

Broussard ran a hand through his hair. 'Because I know why she resigned her position here. You want her back? You need to let me speak to her—so I can explain.'

Something about the man's demeanour caught at Zach's gut. He recognised it. He looked as tortured as Zach felt.

Muttering about ethics, and threatening to do him serious damage if he did anything to hurt or upset Cassandra, Zach scribbled her address on a piece of paper and handed it over. The fact that it was also Ashling's address…that she might be there…was something that stuck under his skin like a thorn.

Broussard left.

Zach put his hands on his table and dropped his

head. Damn. Ashling was even managing to eclipse the fact that his best assistant had resigned for no apparent reason.

The sense that things were beginning to fray badly at the edges of his life was not welcome.

And it only got worse.

After one of the most tumultuous weeks of his life, Zach walked into another exclusive society gathering with a beautiful woman on his arm. The fact that she'd agreed to come with him—she was closely related to the royal family—was proof positive that he'd survived the storm unscathed.

It should be a moment of triumph. But it felt unbelievably hollow—like a lot of other momentous occasions recently.

He couldn't stop his eyes scanning the room. Looking for a splash of colour. A bright blonde head. A flower in hair. A huge open smile.

A stricken, pale face.

The woman beside him tucked her arm into his. He felt like recoiling. He forced a smile. She'd already irritated him by asking him about Ashling—about the identity of the mystery woman who had confronted Henry Field—but thankfully the photographer hadn't caught her face because Zach had stepped in front of her.

It was still all anyone could talk about, though. And it appeared his date wasn't willing to let it go.

She said now, with a little pout that really didn't suit her, 'Honestly, I won't tell a soul. Who was she?'

'She was—' Zach stopped. He'd been about to say

no one, but the words wouldn't form on his tongue. He literally could not voice the lie.

He looked at the woman on his arm. This was it. She was stunning. Perfect. He was on the threshold of everything his mother had wanted for him. The culmination of all the years of work that had precluded his making friends. Having fun. Because it had all been about reaching the ultimate goal.

Walking into a room with the right woman on his arm and being accepted by the very people who would have ground him to dust before he had a chance to speak. The illegitimate son of a cleaning lady.

His mother had been the *wrong* woman, and all she'd wanted for him was *this*. To be standing here with the *right* woman, who would make everything worthwhile.

But he realised now that had been his mother's fight. She'd lived her life through him, bitter and vengeful. She'd blamed Zach for the fact that no man would want to take on a child that wasn't his. But the truth was that she'd never even looked.

'Zach?'

He looked at his date. She was perfect. The right woman. And so wrong.

He extricated her arm from his, said, 'I'm sorry,' and turned and walked out.

'Are you sure you're okay, love? You say those are happy tears, but I know there's something else going on.'

Ashling forced a smile. Of course she couldn't fool her mother, but she really didn't want to distract her today of all days. 'I'm fine, honestly. It's nothing.'

Just a shattered heart.

She pushed her pain aside and hugged her mother. 'I'm so happy for you and Eamon. You deserve this happiness so much. He's so in love with you, it's just…' More tears welled and Ashling had to clamp her mouth shut.

Her mother's partner had rung Ashling during the week, to remind her that it was her mother's fiftieth birthday that weekend and also to ask for Ashling's blessing in his asking for her mother's hand in marriage.

So this evening, while her mother had been celebrating what she'd thought was just a surprise party for her fiftieth, Eamon had got down on one knee and proposed.

Her mother had said yes even before he'd finished speaking.

The surroundings couldn't be more romantic. It was a beautiful garden in the middle of the eco village, just yards from a sandy beach and the wild Atlantic Ocean. Poles had been set around a central area and there were flaming lanterns and fairy lights imbuing the space with a golden glow as the dusk drew in on a long late summer evening.

Children were running free. People were laughing and chatting. Teenagers were building a bonfire on the beach. Music came from the traditional Irish musicians on a makeshift stage. At some point the younger people would moan and complain and start playing more modern music, but not yet.

'Are you sure you're okay?'

Ashling nodded, wiping at her cheeks. She'd tell her mother another time. 'I'm fine. Now, would you please go and celebrate with your fiancé? He's looking lonely over there, surrounded by a hundred people.'

Ashling's mother laughed and went back to Eamon, both of them beaming so hard with happiness they could probably power the national grid. Ashling sighed. She was happy for her mother, truly, she just—

'I have no idea who that man is, but if he's a lost tourist then I am first in line to give him directions. Straight to my bedroom.'

One of Ashling's old schoolfriends, Dervla, had come to stand beside her. She was looking towards the entrance into the village off the main road.

Ashling turned around. And her heart stopped. A man was climbing off a motorbike. He was wearing worn jeans and a leather jacket. Even before he took off his helmet she knew exactly who he was. Her whole body did.

And her heart. That stupid, weak muscle.

Zach was looking around. Bemused. And then he saw her. *Zing*.

Ashling watched him put down the helmet and walk over. He should look ridiculous. A billionaire in an eco-village. Even if he was wearing jeans and a battered leather jacket.

He walked over and stopped in front of her. 'Here you are,' he said, as if it was entirely normal for him to just turn up in the west of Ireland.

Ashling sensed her friend melting away. She barely heard the music and the noise around her. There was a dull roaring in her ears. Blood. Anger. *Desire*.

'Zach.'

His name felt rusty on her tongue. But it had only been a week or so. The longest week of her life. It was as if she had to say his name to make sure this wasn't a hallucination.

'What are you doing here?' She shook her head. 'Did you ride the bike all the way from Dublin?'

'From Dublin Port. Yes.'

That was literally cross-country, about three and a half hours.

His dark gaze swept her up and down, taking in the sundress with its purples and pinks and reds, over which she wore a yellow cardigan, and then all the way down to her yellow wedge sandals.

'You look…colourful.'

Ashling tensed. 'If you've come here just to remind us both how unsuitable I am then—'

He caught her hand. She heard him curse under his breath. He had a look on his face she'd never seen before. Sheepish.

'I'm sorry.'

Ashling pulled her hand back, afraid to have him touch her for fear she'd end up twined around him like a monkey.

'How did you know where to find me?' Her phone had been switched off for days now.

'I went to your apartment. Saw Cassie. She told me—but only after I begged.'

'You begged?'

He nodded. 'I was desperate.'

Ashling's conscience pricked. 'How is Cassie? I left her a phone message, but I didn't see her before I left. I just couldn't…' She trailed off.

She hadn't been able to contemplate seeing her friend and explaining everything that had happened, so she'd left before Cassie had come home.

'She's fine. She's a little preoccupied herself.' Zach's tone was dry.

'With what?'

'The man who followed her to London—Luke Broussard. And the fact that she's resigned.'

'Resigned?'

Zach nodded. He seemed remarkably sanguine about it. 'She said to say that she's sorry she missed the party, but she'll make it up to you and your mother, and that you need to call her ASAP. But you're not to worry and she's fine. And really happy. But she might be moving to America. She'll explain everything when you call.'

Ashling absorbed all that. She was delighted for her friend if everything Zach said was true.

Zach said now, 'Can we go somewhere a little more private to talk?'

Ashling looked around. Dervla and a large contingent of the party guests were subjecting them to serious scrutiny. Ashling didn't want her mother to notice and come over. If she guessed that Zach was the reason behind her tears it wouldn't be pretty.

Ashling led him away from the party to a quieter part of the garden. She faced him. 'What do you want, Zach? Why did you come all the way here?'

'Because I want you.'

Her heart leapt and every cell in her body sizzled with awareness. But she clamped down on her reaction. Wanting wasn't enough. It was temporary. She knew how persuasive Zach could be, so she had to nip this in the bud. Now.

She forced herself to look at him. 'I want you too, Zach. I wanted you from the moment we met four years ago. When you rejected me that evening I took it so personally that I went off-script, which I know probably had a lot to do with my last interaction with my father. But I wouldn't have reacted like that in the first place if I hadn't felt a connection. I've never felt that connection with anyone else,' she went on. 'And I don't think I will, ever again. The thing is, Zach, it's more than just physical for me. It's—'

'I love you.'

'I—' Ashling's mouth shut. She opened it. Shut it again. Opened it. 'What did you say?'

'I said I love you. You say you wanted me four years ago? Well, I think I fell in love with you four years ago. You turned my life upside down in less than two minutes and, as much as I'd have loved to dismiss you, I knew there was more to you than that. That's why I reacted so strongly. Then I couldn't get your face out of my head. I think I looked for you everywhere. And when you arrived that evening, with my tux…' He shook his head. 'You set something alight in me four years ago. You made me question everything I was striving for, even though I wouldn't admit it at the time. It was only when we met again that I had to confront it.'

'Confront what?' Ashling felt as if she was in a dream.

'Confront the fact that I'd been living out my mother's ambition for revenge. She sacrificed her life for me and never let me forget it. She loved me, but she also resented me. Blamed me for a lost life. Look at your mother…getting engaged…finding happiness. She hasn't let bitterness blight her life. Or yours.' Zach shook his head. 'When you stood in front of my father—' He stopped, the colour leaching from his cheeks. 'I've had nightmares about him hitting you, Ash. If he had…he could have—'

Ashling caught Zach's hand. Lifted it up. 'He didn't because you stopped him. I'm sorry again about that…'

Zach shook his head. 'Don't be. You were fearless. I've never seen anything like it.'

'Did it come out in the papers?' Zach nodded and Ashling winced. 'I'm so sorry.'

'Don't be. It was the best thing. Not for him, though. His life has unravelled spectacularly. His wife has accused him of domestic abuse. A legion of women have come out of the woodwork claiming that he fathered their children and paid them off. He's been accused of violence by more than just his wife. His reputation is ruined. But in all honesty I don't even take any pleasure in it. I'm ashamed he's my father, but I feel I can move on now and live my life for *me*. Not to get back at him and not to avenge my mother.'

Emotion made Ashling's chest tight. 'I'm really glad, Zach. You deserve that peace of mind.'

Zach looked serious. 'And you deserve an apology. I'm so sorry for the things I said that evening. For making you wear that dress.'

Ashling let his hand go. 'It was a beautiful dress… just a bit…black and conservative.'

He shook his head. 'It wasn't you. You are not conservative or monochrome.'

There was a beat, and then he said, 'You need to know something. I went to an event last night. I took a woman.'

Ashling went very still.

Zach caught her hands. 'A woman who made me realise that the only woman I wanted with me is *you*.

The first thing I did when we arrived was look for you. For some colour—anywhere. There wasn't any. So I left pretty much as soon as we'd arrived. And now I'm here. Because I want you, Ash. I want colour and I want to live in a world where cynicism isn't the norm.'

'That thing with Elena—'

He put a finger to her mouth. 'Not my business. *Your* business—with her. And if some day it happens that you do something together I'll be there to support you in any way I can.'

Ashling's heart beat fast. 'Some day...? You mean... like in the future?'

Zach smiled. 'I mean...like for the rest of our lives. If you'll have me.'

'Have you as in...?'

'Lover, friend, life partner... Husband. And maybe...when we figure out how we feel about it after our own experiences...children?'

Ashling's head was spinning. She took a breath. 'Zachary Temple, are you telling me that you love me and that you want to marry me and have a family?'

'I actually told you I loved you a couple of minutes ago, but maybe that got lost in—'

Ashling hit him on the arm. She felt suddenly shy. 'I heard you. I just don't think I believed what I was hearing.'

'You heard me right. So now there's only one more thing to ascertain...'

She looked at Zach's mouth, wondering what it would take to get him to stop talking and kiss her.

'Eyes up, Ash.'

She looked at him.

'Do you love me?'

She looked at him in disbelief. Was he completely blind? 'Of course I do. I love you so much but I didn't say it because I thought you just wanted a relationship until things fizzled out, and I knew I couldn't cope with that ultimate rejection and then watch you go on to marry some perfect corporate wife. Because that's what my father did and I just…' She stopped. Sucked in a breath. Then she put her arms around Zach's neck. 'Yes, I love you, Zach Temple. And yes to everything. For ever. *Yes.*'

And then, finally, he kissed her, and didn't stop for a very long time.

EPILOGUE

Five years later, Somerset

'THIS PLACE IS so idyllic, Ash. How can you ever bear to go back to London?'

Ashling grinned at her best friend Cassie, who was sitting on the other side of the table on the terrace. They'd just finished a long, leisurely lunch.

She threw a napkin at her friend, 'Says the woman who has a freaking island!'

Cassie smiled smugly. 'Well, yes, there is that…'

Cassie and her husband Luke Broussard, tech zillionaire, lived mostly on an island off the coast of Oregon in the United States. The place where they'd first fallen in love. They also had a townhouse in San Francisco, for when they needed to attend to their extremely successful corporate lives, not to mention homes in pretty much every other major city in the world, so their family could always have a settled base when they needed to travel.

Just then a mewling sound came from Ashling's breast. She looked down and stroked the downy cheek of her baby girl, Georgie, and helped her to latch on again.

Opposite, her friend was similarly engaged. Except *her* baby girl—Celestine—was a month older. Ashling was already having visions of them being best friends, living together and having adventures...

'You know that Zach thinks we deliberately contrived to have babies at the same time?' Ashling commented wryly.

Cassie laughed. 'Luke may have said something similar.'

'It's not still weird for you, is it? Me and Zach?'

It had taken Cassie a little while to get used to seeing her best friend with her old boss. But she rolled her eyes now. 'Ash, I think I got over it as soon as I saw you together. If ever there was a case of opposites attracting... The thing that freaked me out most was him turning into a man who had actual feelings! Although hearing you call him by his first name for the first time was also a bit of a shock...'

Ashling laughed. She missed her life with her best friend, especially as they lived so far apart now, but they saw each other as much as possible. Each summer here at the country house, for Zach's annual party, and many more times during the year.

Cassie asked now, 'How's the newest studio going?'

Pride filled Ashling. She'd just opened another yoga studio, here in the local village. Elena Stephanides had championed and invested in Ashling's pipedream to open her own business, and her first studio had opened on the ground floor of the Temple Corp headquarters, along with a crèche for its employees.

She had other studios in London now, and one in Athens too. The Stephanides were close, valued friends and godparents to Georgie.

'It's amazing,' she said. 'The locals have really embraced it—' She broke off when she heard shouts from the other end of the garden.

'There goes our peace,' Cassie observed dryly.

Ashling took in the scene. Zach and Luke were walking back from the lake with two small boys on their shoulders—Devin and Louis, their respective sons. The men were dripping wet after their swim in the lake, wearing nothing but board shorts. A view that both women took in with a sigh of very feminine appreciation.

Orla, Devin's non-identical twin sister, ran ahead, holding something small and furry and distinctly wet, that was wriggling in her arms. 'Mum!' she shouted, 'Ziggy had his first swim and he didn't drown!'

Ashling smiled. There went their peace, indeed. But what was coming in its place was so much more satisfying.

Just before the chaos reached her and Cassie they shared a private look. They might relish their moments of peace, but they both relished *this* so much more. It was a life and existence beyond anything either of them could ever have imagined, filled with infinite love.

* * * * *

If you were head over heels for
The Flaw in His Red-Hot Revenge
*make sure to check out the first instalment in
the Hot Summer Nights with a Billionaire duet,*
One Wild Night with Her Enemy *by Heidi Rice.*

Also, don't miss these other stories by Abby Green!

Redeemed by His Stolen Bride
The Greek's Unknown Bride
The Maid's Best Kept Secret
The Innocent Behind the Scandal
Bride Behind the Desert Veil

Available now

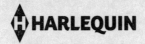

#3941 THE WEDDING NIGHT THEY NEVER HAD
by Jackie Ashenden

As king, Cassius requires a real queen by his side. Not Inara, his wife in name only. But when their unfulfilled desire finally gives her the courage to ask for a true marriage, can Inara be the queen he needs?

#3942 MANHATTAN'S MOST SCANDALOUS REUNION
The Secret Sisters
by Dani Collins

When the paparazzi mistake Nina for a supermodel, she takes refuge in her ex's New York penthouse. Big mistake. She's reminded of just how intensely seductive Reve can be. And how difficult it will be to walk away...again.

#3943 BEAUTY IN THE BILLIONAIRE'S BED
by Louise Fuller

Guarded billionaire Arlo Milburn never expected to find gorgeous stranger Frankie Fox in his bed! While they're stranded on his private island, their intense attraction brings them together... But can it break down his walls entirely?

#3944 THE ONLY KING TO CLAIM HER
The Kings of California
by Millie Adams

Innocent queen Annick knows there are those out there looking to destroy her. Turning to dark-hearted Maximus King is the answer, but she's shocked when he proposes a much more permanent solution—marriage!

YOU CAN FIND MORE INFORMATION ON UPCOMING HARLEQUIN TITLES, FREE EXCERPTS AND MORE AT HARLEQUIN.COM.

HPCNMRB0821